CW00829714

WESTERN WILDFIRE

IFOR WYN WILLIAMS

Translated by Haf Llewelyn

Gwasg Carreg Gwalch

First published in Welsh in 1971, new edition 2021: *Gwres o'r Gorllewin*

ISBN: 978-1-84527-834-2

Published with the financial support of the Books Council of Wales

Cover design: Siôn Ilar
Map: Alison Davies

Published by Gwasg Carreg Gwalch,
12 Iard yr Orsaf, Llanrwst, Dyffryn Conwy, Cymru LL26 0EH.
Tel: 01492 642031
email: llyfrau@carreg-gwalch.cymru
website: www.carreg-gwalch.cymru

Printed and published in Wales

To Owen Wyn

With many happy memories of our time together.
Our endless discussions about Gruffudd ap Cynan,
which planted the seed for translating the original
Welsh novel Gwres or Gorllewin into the English language
so that many more readers could enjoy this novel.

Ifor Wyn Williams

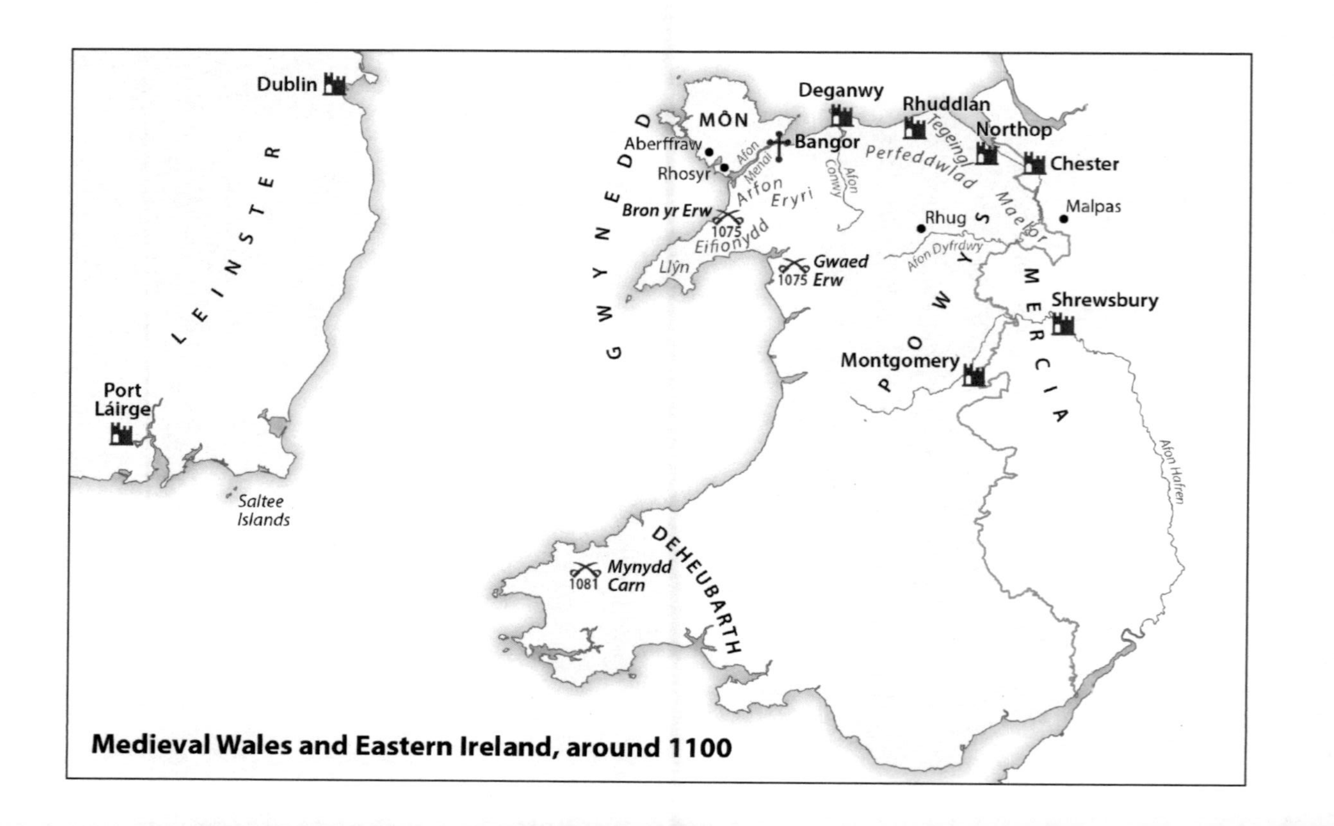

Medieval Wales and Eastern Ireland, around 1100

1

'It was daring of you – coming here.'

She turned to look at Gruffudd. 'Daring? You accuse me of being daring!'

The young man smiled, and took her hand, grasping it a little firmer. They walked in silence, the sand stretching ahead of them.

'You took a risk, Angharad.'

'Just a little.' She stopped, sensing a hint of that strange fierceness in his voice. 'My father came with me.' She turned towards him, suddenly realising his train of thought – 'Is it Rhuddlan?'

'How does my friend Robert fare these days?' His voice strained.

'Dangerous, as always . . . but not impossible to handle.'

He understood her hushed answer. Glancing back, the old woman – her servant, was only a short distance away; they had to be cautious. And behind her, Gruffudd's men followed – Collwyn and three soldiers.

'What is it? Do you not trust her?' he asked.

'It's best that she does not hear.'

'Is she one of Robert's ears?'

'Perhaps . . .'

'But you can handle him?'

'Those were not my words.' Her answer swift.

'You have a way . . .'

'Sometimes.' He noticed the colour rising on her cheeks. Suddenly he was angry. The shell he had lifted with his shoe hurtled along the beach, as he let go of her hand.

'Why, Angharad?'

'Why am I able to appease him? Because he likes me.' She looked at him, almost defying.

'How lovely!'

'No, just useful.'

'Of course – a room of your own – well, almost . . . at the castle . . .'

She turned to face him, glaring. 'It's easy for you to mock me, here on the beach at Aberffraw, it's so tranquil here. You know nothing of life at Tegeingl, it's not like Môn or Arfon, where you have your own people – you don't live beneath the shadow of Rhuddlan castle. Can you imagine what it's like having that fortress towering between you and the open sky – and Chester just a stone's throw away?'

'I can imagine.'

'Oh yes, you can imagine it perhaps, but you don't have to breathe it. I've lived my life bowing to the Normans, just *being* because of their grace; I survive. Have you any idea what that means? No, you don't, because you know nothing of the Normans, you're too preoccupied with fighting your fellow Welshmen.'

Her words hit hard. He could feel his anger rising, and knew he had to defend his actions – but explaining would only show how her words hurt. She already knew that he could not take up arms against the Normans without first securing the seat of Gwynedd as his kingdom.

He walked on, sneaking a glimpse at her; the colour had drained from her face leaving her ashen, her angry words ebbing away from them. She was beautiful, with the sun's glow on her golden hair, the azure of the endless ocean in her eyes – she reminded him of the girls back at the court of the Danes in Dublin. No, she was different, despite her youth – she had a strange strength, a depth that beguiled him, sometimes angering him, as she had today, but sometimes stirring in him a new strength, a determination. She was fairer than the Dublin girls in her blue dress, as beautiful as the lady in Waterford, at the court in Port Láirge . . .

Walking with her on the beach, he started to rue her noble manners. She could not step away from the fact that she was made of better things; she had royalty in her blood. The Dublin girls had no such inhibitions, nothing to hinder their teasing. But in Dublin, he was not king. Here he realised he had a duty, a royal reputation to keep, a dignity that required not only a lover but also a queen . . . He longed to take her in his arms.

'Your golden hair, and your eyes . . .' he whispered, 'Your beauty captivates me, but I'm a very fortunate captive . . .'

She laughed, the lightness returning between them.

'You tease me . . .'

'You travelled all the way from Tegeingl to be teased?'

She stood there; her eyes fixed on the ebbing water.

'No. My father came to meet Gwynedd's new king . . .'

'Yes, and why did you come?'

'Because . . . I wanted to see you.'

He took her hand. 'I'm glad.'

Then he turned to his men, and waved. 'Stay on the beach, we're going looking for gulls' nests!'

Collwyn waved back and nodded; he understood.

Hand in hand, they climbed the dunes.

'Gulls' nests?' she laughed.

'Yes, the gulls that followed a ship into the cove, or so the story goes. Strangely they disappeared for six years, and have only just returned, building their nests once again.'

'Interesting!' she smiled. 'The king is not the only one returning after six years of absence – is it a sign perhaps?'

'I hope so. However, if they left tomorrow – it would mean nothing.'

They climbed further in silence until they reached the spot where the gulls hovered above.

'There!' he pointed. 'And now that we've managed to lose our followers, we need not go any further.' He took his cloak and spread it on the sand. They sat side by side watching the birds soaring out towards the sea. Gruffudd turned to her, and took her hand in his, 'I love you, Angharad.'

She followed the flight of the gulls, silently.

'Well?' Gruffudd, confused at her silence, loosened his hold of her hand. 'Do you hear such words so often that they mean nothing to you?'

'No, but I understand that maybe you have spoken them many times before . . .'

'I . . .'

He didn't want to let the moment turn sour, turn into another quarrel. He forced his voice to stay calm. 'Oh . . . so the gossips have been busy, and you listen to all their stories?'

'Not all – only some that may concern me.'

He had waited two long days for her to come and visit, and he didn't want to waste the precious time he had with her on silly rumours.

'It is true, that when I was in Ireland . . . and here . . . I may have fallen for other girls.'

'Fallen!'

Ignoring the derision in her voice, he added, 'But Angharad, I did not ask any other girl to become my queen.' This was not entirely true, but he alone and the lady in question from the court at Port Láirge would be the only ones who knew – and certain members of her family perhaps.

Angharad's face softened.

'Is that true, Gruffudd?'

He smiled. 'Sometimes it's difficult for a man who risks his life for his kingship to live a . . .' He looked for the word that translated to 'restrained', but thought better of it – '. . . to live wisely.'

'Ah yes – a hero's privilege,' she said, softly.

'Something like that.' He paused. 'And do you forgive?'

'I have no choice,' Angharad sighed. 'You are . . . well, a hero . . .'

'Is that how you look at me?'

'Of course . . . over the past seven years, there has been no one but you.'

Gruffudd could feel her fingers gripping his, soft and warm.

'Do you remember the first time I saw you? You wore a blue dress that day . . .'

'It was green!' She laughed, lighter now.

'And your hair, it tumbled over your shoulders, not tucked under a bonnet or cowl.'

'It was held back by a gold band!'

'I didn't see it – in the midst of all that brightness!'

'I'd worn it to impress the new king, and you didn't notice!' She held on to his arm. 'And you – I'll never forget the moment when you entered the court, with six giant Danes guarding you – you seemed so fierce – as if you intended to conquer Rhuddlan castle that very evening!'

'I don't deny, it had crossed my mind – no wonder Robert agreed to help me.'

They both laughed, the gulls watching from afar.

'And that axe you had, waving it as you spoke . . . making everyone nervous . . .'

'It was a mistake . . .' He looked once again for the correct word. 'It didn't help matters, giving the impression that I was more of a Dane, not a true Welshman.'

'You were young,' she submitted.

'Yes, just twenty-one, and reckless!'

She looked at him, and smiled. 'Don't be too harsh on yourself, there is no other man like you in the whole country. Your Welsh, though,' she laughed, 'back then, it was the strangest Welsh I'd ever heard!'

It was clear that his humility had had the right effect on her.

'I must have said strange things without thinking sometimes.'

'Oh yes!' Angharad was shaking with laughter. 'Do you remember asking me, very seriously, as soon as we met –

Are you a Welshman?'

They both laughed. 'Believe me, it was my Welsh that was at fault and not my eyes.' He looked at her admiringly. 'I would have to be blind to make such a mistake again.' Relieved, he raised her fingers to his lips, the tension between them melting away.

'Gruffudd,' her voice tender. 'Gruffudd . . . *Gwres o'r Gorllewin* – the western spirit that rekindles the flame.'

'What?'

'That's what Baron Robert of Rhuddlan calls you . . . *Gwres o'r Gorllewin* – Western Wildfire.'

'Oh!' Why had she dragged the Norman's name into the conversation again? Was it teasing? Goading?

Even if it was just an innocent comment, it was clear – the Norman was in her thoughts . . . Gruffudd forced his voice to be reasonable – 'Robert has named me well.'

'Oh yes,' she smiled. 'But he had another name for you when you returned to Rhuddlan following the battle at Gwaed Erw, when you set fire to the castle . . .' She watched him. 'You won't be offended?'

He shook his head.

'The pirate!'

But the name did offend. It was the name given him by the men of Llŷn and Eifionydd when they rose against him at Bron-yr-Erw. He deserved better; the name should have been forgotten – after seven years of effort and eventually securing the throne of Gwynedd. He felt certain now that she was trying to hurt him; an innocent comment would never be so accurate. He stared at her.

'Never use that name again.'

He dropped her hands.

'How dare you ridicule me in this way? You playing with my feelings as if I were the son of a serf, a nobody . . .' He laughed sadly. 'And did you not realize why I came back to Rhuddlan from that battle at Gwaed Erw?'

Suddenly she was pressing her face into his shoulder. 'Gruffudd, I'm sorry, I had to hurt you . . .' She fought back the tears. 'I had to punish you . . . because I have to punish myself!'

Gruffudd fought the urge to take her in his arms, press her to him and whisper comforting words. He kept his voice cold.

'Punish yourself? Why, Angharad?'

'I failed myself . . . and failed you.' Her voice was low, her hands covering her face.

'How?'

'I lost faith in you. I regret what I have become. I am ashamed of how accustomed I have become to their ways. I've *had* to depend on the friendship of the Normans, or perhaps I've just accepted it.'

He didn't want to know more about the 'friendship'. It would be wiser to accept her remorse, and convince her of his love for her. Slowly, he raised his arms and drew her to him, kissing her hair. 'Six years ago, I asked you to become my wife, one day . . . I still love you.'

'Are your words sincere?'

'I think you know the answer . . .' He kissed her softly.

'Yes . . .' her eyes serious.

'And you?'

'The last six years have been difficult . . . because of my feelings for you,' she looked away, 'but I'm afraid that I will suffer again because of my love for you.'

'You are afraid that I will leave you again?'

'Yes, the more love I have for you, the more hurt I will face . . . it will destroy me.'

'You will not lose me – ever. I have a throne, my enemy Trahaearn is dead, the men of Môn, Arfon and Llŷn are behind *me* now.'

Angharad touched the scar with the tip of her finger – the scar that ran from below his ear towards the nape of his neck.

'Gruffudd, you are just like all of us. That scar – it almost took you away from me.'

'Ha! It was his last strike – one of Trahaearn's men, slain on Mynydd Carn.' He laughed. 'God has given me the strength of an oak, I have the might of two men in my arms!' He stopped, knowing that he was slipping into his old habit – boasting – but it was the truth.

'I know, letting you take me in your arms is always a risk!'

'Did I hurt you?'

'It's a sweet pain.'

'Don't worry about my scars, or losing me, Angharad. Heaven watches over me, one of the saints – Saint Columba, perhaps – is protecting me. It must be so, otherwise I would not be here. I've been too near death so many times, something or someone must be looking out for me.' He smiled playfully. 'It might be the spirits of those old Danes – my heathen ancestors.' Pride and determination filled his voice. 'I'm a king, Angharad – I'm the rightful King of Gwynedd

– I shall be a just king; not a single soul will daunt me.'

Gruffudd, aware once more of the screeching gulls overhead, the faraway sound of the tide returning, the wind rustling in the reeds, breathed in the scent of the sun warming her skin.

Angharad turned her face towards his. 'I shall believe that heaven will protect you.'

'And so, you will love me more than ever?'

'Yes,' she whispered.

Suddenly he felt wary. For days he had prepared the question, but now, he felt a strange fear. He looked around, as if seeing the sights for the first time. 'Aberffraw – it is easy to feel fondness for this place.'

'Yes, it's a haven.'

This was his chance, he had to ask. 'Well – would you be happy here? Will you join me here at the court, as my queen? Queen of the court of Aberffraw?'

'Are you asking me to marry you?' She paused, the colour rising once more.

'Of course! Well, will you become my wife?'

'I will.'

Gruffudd bowed and kissed her forehead. His lips finding her warm mouth, he took her in his arms, holding her tightly. Suddenly he loosened his arms, fearful. 'Did I hurt you?'

'No, I will only be hurt when you're not there to hold me.'

They rose, time had stopped, they should return to court.

'I will ask your father. I must do this correctly . . .'

They returned over the dunes, hand in hand, Angharad silent, thinking ahead of her father, there at court, waiting.

'What are you thinking?'

'Don't be cross Gruffudd – do you promise?'

Suddenly his fears returned. 'What is it?'

'Don't tell anyone of our marriage. You must believe me when I say that I love you, every sinew in my body loves you – and I will not prove happiness until I can become your wife – but don't tell my father, or anyone else, of our plan, yet.'

'But he's here now – it's a perfect opportunity.'

'We'll come and visit in a month or so.'

'But there are plans to be made, things to organise; I want you here as my queen before Christmas.'

'I will be here, I promise, but for now it's wisest to keep it a secret.'

As he helped her over the last dune, he spat the word into the sea spray – 'Wise!' Then he added quietly, 'But one day I will kill him!'

She bowed her head.

'In a month's time, or two, whatever suits you – everyone will know that you will be my queen – Gwynedd, the Welsh and the Normans – everyone must hear!'

'Even the Irish?' she teased. He gazed at her, then laughed.

'Yes, the Irish will know. But if I have to, I'll come and escort you from your father's house in Tegeingl.' He looked into her eyes, his face set – 'Or from Rhuddlan castle, if I must.'

She met his gaze. 'I have no doubt.'

2

Two weeks had passed – Angharad and her father Owain ab Edwin had returned to Tegeingl. Despite his duties in those early days on the throne, Gruffudd's thoughts often returned to Angharad and the visit. Her beauty and youth, her dignity and tenderness evoked a longing in him. Beneath her beauty there was also a strength that had enthralled him, an assurance about her – a stubbornness perhaps. She would be a fine queen . . .

Only occasionally would his thoughts turn to Máire, the lady at Port Láirge, bringing with them an unease – a strange apprehension. But he had made his choice.

Angharad's position at Tegeingl – a rose between the two Norman thorns – was never far from his thoughts. It made him uneasy; she was vulnerable, positioned between the two Norman cousins Hugh the Earl of Chester, and Robert, Lord of Rhuddlan. Of the two, it was always Robert that had been a threat, setting his sights firmly on Angharad and the throne of Gwynedd. During their recent visit, it had become increasingly obvious that her father was at the mercy of Robert. It had become more apparent on their last evening at Aberffraw. Earlier that day, Owain's son Goronwy had arrived, followed by a company of soldiers. He had come to pay tribute to the new King of Gwynedd, and to escort his father and sister on their journey home. But Gruffudd had immediately taken a dislike to him – his rough voice, echoing his father's, his watery blue eyes which held no trust. Owain had soldiers to escort him and his precious daughter home over the River Clwyd, without having to depend on his son for protection. Why, if he was so eager to pay tribute, had he not come in the same company as his father Owain, and his sister?

Gruffudd suspected that there was another reason. Was he sent by Hugh or Robert? And if so, why? Was it to ensure Angharad's return? Had the son a message for his father? Gruffudd recalled the advice given him by Owain that evening – advice on how to live at peace with the Normans.

'My lord, they are our neighbours and we must learn to live with them . . . not under them, you understand. We must live side by side, and learn to keep our self-esteem.'

Gruffudd had looked at Angharad, but could find no hint of her feelings. However, her brother had nodded earnestly, as his father continued in his rasping voice, 'They have strength, my lord – and they can display terrible cruelty if provoked, but they are fair and just . . . they are dutiful in their faith, and respect our culture – our poets – oh how they hail our poets! They are not heathens like the Dane . . .'

Realising his mistake, he tried to make light of his words, but Gruffudd was grim-faced. Goronwy pitched in, trying to help his father out. 'My father remembers the old Danes, during the reign of Rhodri the Great, Rhodri *Fawr*,' smirking almost. 'Did you know, my lord, that our family has links with Rhodri Fawr?'

Gruffudd ignored this new trail. 'Do they not steal land from under your noses?'

'Not exactly . . .' the father uttered slowly.

'But you are heavily taxed, are you not, on anything of any worth – levied? Even your rights?'

'No,' ventured Goronwy. 'Not everything comes under scrutiny.'

His father went on – one raspy voice followed by the other. 'They are our keepers; they defend our land. The price of their taxes is far less than the cost to us of keeping an army.'

Gruffudd struggled to keep the contempt from his voice. 'You have no army – the baron has taken your best soldiers.'

'As my father wisely said, we have no need for soldiers,' said Goronwy.

'The King of Gwynedd needs soldiers.'

Silence followed.

Then Owain leaned towards the young king. 'Surely, the King of Gwynedd can appreciate that it is wise at times to accommodate neighbours . . . especially mightier neighbours with a taste for war.'

Father and son both smiled. Angharad raised her cup, and Gruffudd remembered the worry in her eyes. Gruffudd had turned to her father –

'And that, Owain ab Edwin, is the best advice you can give the King of Gwynedd?'

'Yes, my lord; we must keep them happy.'

Gruffudd looked from father to son.

'I agree – it would be best for your kingdom.'

'And best for the Normans?' Gruffudd asked. He could not

recall Goronwy's response, but he remembered how Owain had praised Robert of Rhuddlan; that he had been a loyal friend. Then Owain had turned to Angharad.

'My daughter, tell the king how Robert has forgiven his act of torching Rhuddlan castle all those years ago.'

The three men had looked at Angharad, waiting.

She turned towards Gruffudd. 'I have heard him say as much . . .'

Gruffudd watched her, amused. 'What is your advice?'

He watched the faint smile. 'I'm just a young girl – what should I tell you? All I can say is: be vigilant, my lord.'

Owain ab Edwin had emphasized the benefits of working with the Normans. But Gruffudd disliked the whole idea. Especially when he heard that Robert was keen to build a castle in Deganwy. He could not regard Robert's men as strong neighbours, to be respected, but rather as his greatest enemies. The worst of them for many reasons was Robert. The idea had become more apparent to him recently: he must get rid of him. Either that, or they would have to come to an agreement that ensured that the whole of Gwynedd remained free of the Normans.

That evening, a fortnight after Angharad had left, Gruffudd was on his way home to Aberffraw. It was a beautiful evening. Behind him rode fifteen of his best knights on horseback, with Sitriuc the giant from Dublin leading. Following them, a company of sixty soldiers, armed. Over half were Welshmen; the rest – Irish and Danes.

He was flanked on one side by one of his most faithful

lords, Gwyncu, who had been given the prestigious job of supervising the royal house and army of Aberffraw – the *penteulu*. And on his other flank was Collwyn, his faithful companion.

They were returning from their three-day visit to the lords of Arfon and Llŷn. Everywhere he noted with sadness the pillage and plunder left following the terrible campaigns of his enemies – the Normans of course, but also the men of Trahaearn ap Caradog.

They rode in silence, his thoughts troubled by the tales of destruction, homes demolished, lives destroyed.

'I should have returned sooner,' he blurted.

Collwyn turned to him. 'It wasn't your fault.'

'Who was at fault then? My people have suffered.'

'You were welcomed by them all,' added Gwyncu.

'Their welcome and their joy when we came, will stay with me . . . they have faith in me . . . I don't.'

He stopped. He shouldn't voice his doubts – he had a responsibility. He couldn't talk of his fears; Gwyncu was there, an officer. Airing his doubts when it was just Collwyn and himself was a different matter. Collwyn was an old and trusted friend. He had even told Collwyn of his intention to marry Angharad. Collwyn alone knew. The two were close friends, almost brothers. Collwyn was the son of a Welshman, one of the knights who had fled, exiled from Gwynedd to Ireland with Cynan ab Iago, Gruffudd's father.

When Cynan had died, the task of *teaching* Welsh to his young son was transferred to Collwyn's father and, a little later, to Collwyn himself. The two boys grew up in the school of Sord-Cholum-Cille, near Dublin. Both young men had found lovers among the ladies of the courts of Dublin and Port Láirge. Even in the struggles and skirmishes between the Irish and Danes, Collwyn was always at his side, his sword ready. He had put his life on the line at several battles, at Gwaed Erw, and Bron-yr-erw. He had remained a loyal companion when Gruffudd had visited court after court in Ireland, looking for backing for his third campaign to regain Gwynedd. When victory came after the battle of Mynydd Carn two months ago, Collwyn was there. The scars were still visible on his arms, his left shoulder paralysed.

Gruffudd smiled. 'They look on me as if I were one of their saints . . . they have faith.'

From behind him he could sense that the journey had taken its toll on the men – an Irish knight urging the foot-soldiers on. He turned to Gwyncu – 'Tell them to rest, we'll stop for a while, before going on to Rhosyr.'

Gwyncu turned his steed. 'Hold your horses!' He looked at the sun, as it dipped westward, holding its warmth. 'Will we be in Aberffraw by sunset?'

'Yes, the marsh is still dry enough – we won't have trouble crossing.'

By the time they had reached the ridge at Rhosyr, crossed the marsh, and come up through the wooded slope out onto the open moorland, where they could see the royal court of Aberffraw in the distance almost hidden by the dunes, the sun was sinking. There on the horizon a ship appeared.

'Well?' Collwyn nudged his steed towards Gruffudd.

'Arriving in time for tonight's feast,' replied Gruffudd. 'The sentinel will have seen it and deemed that it's come from Ireland. They will be preparing for the visitors at court.'

Collwyn glanced at Gwyncu. He was speaking with one of the Welsh knights. 'What if the ship hails from Port Láirge?'

'Well?' Gruffudd understood his friend's concern.

'What if Máire is on it?' Collwyn continued lightly. 'Or perhaps one of her brothers . . . the fierce one . . . come to see if his sister has been so easily forgotten?'

Gruffudd didn't answer. Máire, of course, could be a problem. Máire – from the court of Port Láirge – she was beautiful. As beautiful as Angharad? Not as stubborn as Angharad perhaps, and a little less reserved. Angharad had a strength in her that Máire could not challenge.

He had promised Máire, between kisses, that she would one day become his wife when he had secured his throne, but he had never told her that she was not his first choice as queen. The Irish knew nothing of Angharad; it was still early, they did not need to know yet. He had to be cautious – what if Angharad refused him? What if her father, or Robert, managed to come between them? It was paramount that he did not offend Máire's father, the King of east Leinster: it was he who had supported Gruffudd's third campaign, and had pledged further support if needed.

'Yes,' Gruffudd smiled. 'Angharad urged me, before she left – I must be vigilant.'

'Or put up with two wives!' They both laughed.

'I'll wait until I find out who is on the ship – then I'll start to worry.' Then turning to Collwyn, his face serious, he added, 'I have more pressing concerns . . . far more unsettling.'

'The state of your people? The harm done to Arfon and Llŷn?'

'I cannot forgive – they must pay for the . . .' He could not find the correct word.

'Violation?'

Gruffudd continued. 'Yes, there must be retribution. My people expect justice.'

'Trahaearn has been killed, and you have already punished Powys.'

'He was a puppet, Trahaearn, trying to appease his masters by leading them through Gwynedd. His masters . . . they must suffer.'

Unexpectedly, a bee whirred between the horse's ears. The creature jerked its head, alarmed.

'This one hasn't the making of a war-horse,' remarked Gruffudd, pulling at the harness, irritated.

Collwyn looked at his friend. 'Perhaps it would be wise to secure your position with the people of Gwynedd, before kicking the Norman hive?'

'I may be forced to attack. They cannot be allowed to go ahead with their plan. A castle in Deganwy will not stand.'

'They may fear you, Gruffudd,' smiled Collwyn. 'What will you do if they recognise your position as the King of Gwynedd, and want peace?'

Gruffudd paused. 'I don't think that will happen, but it's a good question – not the first today, Collwyn!'

The path dropped, and Gruffudd had one last glimpse of the ship before the sea disappeared from view. He could tell by its position that the vessel was bound for Aberffraw.

3

Gruffudd and his men had feasted. The ship was anchored on the shore below the court of Aberffraw, forgotten. Gruffudd had been informed that he had other guests – two noblemen from Edeyrnion, bringing a message from the Normans, requesting a meeting between the Norman barons and Gruffudd.

He'd refused to discuss the matter at first, choosing to join his men at the table. Throughout the banter, the feasting and drinking, despite giving the crippled bard his full attention, his troubled mind crept back to the two noblemen and their message.

The Lord of Edeyrnion, Meirion Goch, sat at his table. Gruffudd regarded him, trying to decide if he was to be trusted. Was it just an unfortunate trait that his eyes would not stay still, darting here and there? Was it nervousness? His face was narrow, his wide mouth a smirk; then there was the reddish beard – Gruffudd didn't like the look of the man. But then, he could of course name more than a few fine-looking men – all of them traitors. He would let them feast, before the questioning.

Soon, the mead had done its work. Gruffudd watched as several of the men pushed the remnants away, and rested their heads on the table. He ushered his council, Collwyn and

Gwyncu and two of his sharpest, most trustworthy advisers, Anarawd and Bleddyn, to his private hall. He invited Meirion Goch and his companion to join them.

'Give me your message once more Meirion – word for word.' He spoke slowly. 'And I advise you to be wise. Tell me the message as it was given, truthfully.'

'I am wise enough to be honest with *you*, my lord king.'

'Go on.'

'Two of the Marcher lords send you their regards. They also ask for your company, and that of the Irish and Danes, at a conference – a peaceful meeting, to be held in Rhug, Edeyrnion.'

'The two lords – they are the barons of Chester and Shrewsbury?'

'Yes my lord, Hugh, Earl of Chester, and Roger of Shrewsbury.'

Gruffudd noted how the man pronounced the men's names, giving them his full respect.

'Anyone else?'

'Of course, knights and foot soldiers.'

The absence of one name was too apparent. Gruffudd repeated his question, impatiently.

'Who else will be there?'

'I don't know, my lord.'

Gruffudd got up abruptly.

'Do you take me for a fool? Answer my question truthfully. Tell me!'

The red headed man kept his eyes on Gruffudd, and when his answer came, his voice was steady. 'Robert of Rhuddlan *may* be present.'

'Of course,' Gruffudd laughed, 'and why keep this name, this . . . name from me?' His voice was full of scorn and disdain. He couldn't find the correct word. He looked at Collwyn.

'This *distinguished* name, perhaps? Was that the word you were after my lord – *distinguished*?' Collwyn struggled to keep the amusement from his voice.

Gruffudd nodded, then turned to the visitor. 'Why keep that *distinguished* name from me?'

'He *may* be there, my lord king, I don't know for certain that he will be present.'

Sitting back in his chair, Gruffudd declared, 'He will be there.'

They all sat for a while in silence, then Gruffudd turned to the second visitor, a tall, towering man. 'Was I given your name?'

'My lord king, my given name is Cynwrig Hir.'

This man's face was open; he seemed more trustworthy.

'Are you this man's friend?'

'We are neighbours, my lord.'

A clever answer, Gruffudd mused – elusive. However, he would not be able to dodge Gruffudd's next question. 'Is he telling me the truth?'

A moment's silence. 'Yes my lord, I would not be here otherwise.'

It was an answer that pleased Gruffudd. 'Is this the true intent of the barons? Peace?'

'As far as I know, sir.'

Did this man have doubts? Another indication of his honesty?

'And how much *do* you know?' Gruffudd asked quickly. 'Apart from what you have been told by your . . . neighbour here?'

The tall man considered the question, again taking his time, before replying. 'I understand that the Norman barons are ready to acknowledge you as King of Gwynedd, my lord. They wish to meet with you on friendly terms . . . as an important neighbour . . .'

Somehow, the message sounded more trustworthy coming from this man.

'This conference – whose idea was it? Which of the barons decided to call the meeting?'

'I don't know, my lord.'

Gruffudd looked at Meirion Goch.

'I cannot be certain . . .'

'Is there anything you do know for certain?' This man's manner irritated Gruffudd – was he being unfair?

'It is my guess that Hugh, Earl of Chester decided on the meeting.'

There was nothing more he could glean from the two visitors. A servant was called; they would be given a bed for the night. When the two had returned to the hall, he turned to his council.

'Give me your thoughts. Gwyncu?'

'My lord, a period of peace is paramount now, your kingdom needs stability and you must gather strength in order to become a stable force in Gwynedd.'

'I agree,' Collwyn concurred.

Gruffudd thought for a moment, before turning to his

aging counsellor. 'Yes. But what do you say Anarawd?'

'I agree, of course – you must gain peace, then you can strengthen your grip here. But it is not as you two think . . .' he stopped, raising his hand to his beard, a habit of his when he felt he had shrewd advice to share. 'If this is clear to us – the route we should take, then surely it will also be clear to any astute Norman. It's very unlikely that they are contemplating letting you have time to strengthen your army and sort out your kingdom.'

'Your words make sense. Bleddyn?'

Gruffudd knew how Bleddyn liked to disagree with the older councillor. They were always competitive, the two men – the young and the old – each willing the king to come down in favour of his advice. Bleddyn was much travelled, he knew the Welsh kingdoms and their battles with the Norman enemy. Gruffudd suspected that the younger man often argued solely to display his knowledge. However, when both councillors agreed, Gruffudd knew that their judgement was wise, and that he should heed their advice. Just now he hoped that Bleddyn agreed.

'My lord, I disagree with my wise friend Anarawd. I fear his reasoning this time is rather . . . obvious.'

Gruffudd, taken aback – he had, after all, praised the older man's thinking – abruptly replied, 'Oh? How is that?'

'My lord, *his* mistake . . .' – Gruffudd noted the emphasis – 'is to think that the Normans believe that you are in a weak position. They are impressed by your fatal victory over Trahaearn. I know what you think of Trahaearn, I know the feelings of this court, and of those who suffered because of him. The whole of Gwynedd despises him. But he was an efficient ruler – he was the King of Powys and as king he kept the Normans out of his kingdom. The Normans showed him respect, so much so that they kept to the treaty that was made between them.' Bleddyn smiled, then continued. 'How much more respect must they have then, towards you – you who defeated the great Trahaearn? Think how keen they must be to settle a peace treaty with you.'

Gruffudd regarded Bleddyn's argument. It was logical enough . . . but the Normans, they couldn't be trusted. They had ransacked and plundered his land throughout his time in exile, while he waited for his chance to return from Ireland. They hadn't stopped at Tegeingl, they had taken the whole of Perfeddwlad – the Welsh Midlands. It was Robert of Rhuddlan who had it all planned, the taking of Perfeddwlad, and the building of the castle at Deganwy. Was this all part of Robert's great plan? The castle at Chester taking the lands around Tegeingl, the castle at Rhuddlan capturing Perfeddwlad and subsequently a castle at Deganwy so that they could cross the river Conwy and take Gwynedd? . . . But Trahaearn had won their respect, his kingdom was not attacked . . .

Gruffudd needed time, he had to strengthen his army and the will of his people first, then perhaps he could resist the inevitable attack.

'Gwyncu, can we assemble an army, strong enough to face the might of the barons? Do we have the men now?'

'All three barons?'

'Yes.'

'If we had six months perhaps . . .' By then, Gruffudd mused, Angharad would be here as his wife. Gwyncu went on, 'But perhaps with the backing of the Irish?'

The ship! It should have reached the estuary, unless it was heading further – towards the Menai perhaps. His mind was uneasy, a sure sign of his dilemma. He straightened his back, sitting up in his chair. 'No, I can't ask the Irish for further support, not now – half of my army are already Irishmen.'

He knew that he had already leaned too heavily on the Irish and Danes; he could not have done without them. And their presence, having them around him, was a constant comfort.

Suddenly, he was aware of his council waiting, watching him.

'It seems then that I don't have the strength at present to fight the barons. Gwyncu, I agree with you – we need six months. I have a choice: I can accept this offer of friendship, which will give us time to strengthen, or . . . we refuse. That would mean war.' He smiled. 'A difficult choice.' He got to his feet and nodded, 'I will decide, and give you my answer in the morning'.

The council moved towards the heavy curtain dividing the room. Gwyncu turned to face the king. 'Sir, there is one matter which puzzles me – the Normans . . .'

Gruffudd knew what was coming; he had hoped that it would not be raised. The Normans had asked for his attendance, and had expressly asked for the presence of the Danes and Irish – but not the Welsh.

'Why do the Normans want you to take the soldiers from Ireland and not the Welsh . . .'

A voice bellowed from beyond the curtain. 'My lord king!'

'What is it Sitriuc?'

'A ship, an Irish ship . . . in the bay.'

'Ireland?'

'Yes, from Port Láirge, Máire's brothers are here my lord!'

Gruffudd glanced towards Collwyn. His friend smiled.

'Is it just the two brothers, Sitriuc?'

'No sir, there are three of them, and they want to see you.'

Three. The number was relevant – this was not a mere social visit.

From the great hall, he could hear the cheers; the Danes at least were glad of their presence. Then Gruffudd heard Sitriuc's roar – they were old friends.

Gruffudd turned to his Welsh council, his mind elsewhere. 'I'll think of the matter we discussed . . . the Norman request, but now I must welcome our latest guests. They are the sons of Leinster's king, who gave me his support. We must show them our greatest respect. Gwyncu, will you go to them? They must have a room of their own . . . I will join you soon.'

Alone, Gruffudd looked through the narrow slit of a window. He could just make out the shapes of the dunes and the light on the river beyond. A lonely gull gave out a cry somewhere above the stretch of sea. Gruffudd suddenly felt a weight pressing down on him: it was he alone who had decisions to make. A loneliness came with responsibility. He could lead an army or fleet, but leading a kingdom was a different matter. Caution, as opposed to certainty of attack, made him uneasy . . .

He became aware of a cluster of trees not far from the

court, their shadow a fortress guarding the marsh, watching the sea. The horizon had melted away, dusk was folding in on the estuary, but he could still make out the contour of the hills towards Arfon, and there in the distance he could just make out the lights of fires dotted here and there – beacons on far off greying hills.

Further still, beyond the mountains, was Rhug. He knew that the decision would be just as difficult in the morning, in a week's time, in a month, there was no way out. Any decision he made would be akin to staring along the blade of a sword – whichever angle he took.

Down below he watched as a group of men struggled with the sail of the ship. He felt the unease within him stir again – he didn't like the three brothers; he knew how they had tried to stop their father from giving him their support in the form of ships and soldiers. After he had established himself at the court in Aberffraw, all the ships and some of the soldiers had returned to Leinster.

Had the three come on friendly terms? Had they come to force him to keep his word? He had, after all, promised to make Máire, their sister, his wife. If challenged, what was he to do? If he failed to honour his promise, they could order ships from Leinster – if the Danes and Irish returned it would leave him with just a dwindled and weak army. He could not let that happen. He had great respect for the King of Leinster, but he also knew that his wife of choice was Angharad; he wanted her with him in Aberffraw.

He pressed his head against the cool granite of the window frame, his conflicting thoughts mirroring the blurred shapes of dusk outside. Only one certainty remained – he needed time to gather a powerful army in Gwynedd; he needed time to gain strength in his new kingdom, gain the confidence of his people. With his own men behind him, his reliance on Port Láirge would end. He would then be free to make Angharad rather than Máire his queen, without fear of the outcome. Then he could expect more than just respect from the Normans.

He hurried to the great hall, greeted the three brothers warmly, and sat with them at the table while they feasted. Later, in his private room, with Collwyn by his side, he faced the three brothers. Politely he questioned them – Was their father well? How were his campaigns against the Irish? How did the Danes at Dublin fare? Was everything in order in Port Láirge; the court attendants – were they well? And Máire?

She was well, they said, yearned for him, of course, and as beautiful as ever.

Gruffudd smiled, remembering Collwyn's suggestion of taking two wives. Olaf, the elder brother nodded.

'We came, of course, to pay tribute to you as a new king – once more. But we also have an important issue we need to raise . . . and arrange . . .'

'Máire?'

'Yes.'

'She is constantly in my thoughts . . .' confidently. He wasn't lying, he often thought of Máire. 'I long for her every day. But . . .'

'But?'

'When your sister comes to Aberffraw, then there must be

no question as to her safety . . . she must be welcomed to a secure kingdom.'

'True, but you have secured your kingdom, have you not?'

Gruffudd noted how this man, a prince, could not honour him with a title – no *my lord* or *king*. The time would come when he would demand respect. Lightly, he added, 'Have you ever encountered the Normans?'

'No, why?'

'They would take my kingdom from me.'

Olaf frowned. 'Is this true?'

'They have summoned me and the soldiers that came from Ireland, to a meeting . . .' Gruffudd paused: he had a playful thought. 'You come from Ireland. The Normans would welcome you . . .'

'But we aren't your soldiers,' Olaf replied, bitingly.

'Scared?'

Gruffudd knew them well. Their reaction was just as he'd guessed. The largest of the men, the one Collwyn had so aptly described, stood up.

'When did you see me afraid, eh?'

'Sit down.' The giant stayed on his feet, towering, sitting only when motioned to do so by Olaf. Gruffudd continued, 'It would be an opportunity for you, as your sister's protectors, to see for yourselves the power of the Normans. You will then realise the danger they pose to Gwynedd.'

Slowly a decision was forming in his mind. If he took the risk of meeting the Normans in Rhug, then he would take the three brothers with him, and their men, together with his army. They would be useful if trouble broke out.

'You are not afraid to face the Normans?' Olaf's voice challenged him.

'The *king* has decided.' Collwyn spoke, his voice lowered.

Olaf's eyes fixed on Gruffudd. 'To do what exactly?'

Gruffudd smiled. 'You know me well Olaf – I will go to Rhug, and you will accompany me.'

Olaf glanced uncertainly at his two brothers. 'Of course,' he replied. 'It will be most interesting.'

4

As they got nearer the meeting place at Rhug, Gruffudd's unease grew. He took some comfort in the agility and strength of the chestnut stallion, his new horse. He watched the path, eyes alert to any danger. At his side was Collwyn, and a further hundred yards or so in front, Meirion Goch and Cynwrig Hir led the way. Following Gruffudd on three ebony steeds rode the brothers, and behind them, Sitriuc and the other knights, followed by foot-soldiers.

Leading a company of over four hundred men, Gruffudd was aware that all the men were born in Ireland; he had no Welsh soldiers backing him.

Two days earlier they had left Aberffraw, leaving Gwyncu in charge of the royal court and the Welsh army. As the sun set on the first day, somewhere in the midst of the Eryri mountains, they had reached a stream running from a steep ridge, and that evening they had made camp on the edge of a river in the cantref of Rhufoniog, not far from Rhug, so that they could get to the meeting by early morning, refreshed.

The path, Gruffudd noticed, was steadily rising up a steep, tree-lined slope, avoiding marshland. Slowing his horse, not wishing to hurry the soldiers uphill, he called Collwyn to his side.

'Call Meirion Goch back.' A curlew hurtled from the marsh, alarmed.

The redheaded man turned his horse and returned to where Gruffudd had slowed down.

'How far have we to go?'

'Two miles, my lord, less than an hour.'

'Does the path go through those trees?'

'Yes, my lord. It follows this hill, up through the trees and then down towards the valley and the river Dee. It's a wide valley. The two earls will be waiting there, with their men, near the river.'

'Do these trees surround the valley?'

Gruffudd watched as the man's lips seemed to move, forming silent words – uncertain how to answer.

'I'm . . . I don't know, my lord.'

Gruffudd scowled. 'Search your memory . . .'

'On two sides . . . perhaps.'

'Just two sides?'

Meirion Goch eyed the young king. 'Just two sides, my lord.'

'You can go back to your position – lead on.'

'Every time I talk to that man, I feel less sure of this journey.' He watched as Meirion Goch returned to the front.

'Why don't you ask the other man?'

'He's honest, but kept in the dark. He knows nothing of the arrangements.'

'Do you fear that they may have men in the trees?'

Gruffudd peered uphill towards the summit and the edge of the forest. 'Yes, we must be . . .'

Again, the correct word eluded him; he turned to Collwyn and finished his sentence in the language of the Danes, 'we must be vigilant once we reach the edge of those trees . . .'

Collwyn smiled, but continued in Welsh, 'It's not too late. You can change your mind; we can turn back.'

'No – it's far too late for a king to turn back.' Turning back to Welsh, he spoke quickly now. 'Tell Sitriuc to give the command – everyone must be ready, they must have their weapons at hand, tell him to call twelve of the knights – they should go ahead, between us and those two.'

As they rode slowly through the forest, a long line of horses and men, the eldest of the brothers rode up to Gruffudd. 'Are we nearing the place where the Normans are waiting?'

'Yes, almost there.' Not taking his eyes off the path.

'Well, forgive my intrusion, but is it wise to arrive at a peaceful meeting, weapons ready – as if we were going into battle?'

'Yes, it's wise,' was the blunt reply, 'and forgive me *my* intrusion – stay with your brothers! When I need advice, I'll let you know.'

Olaf smiled scornfully, and Gruffudd had to stifle the urge to push the man off his horse.

'Go!' he yelled. 'Now!'

The last stage of their journey, just an hour before arriving at Rhug, was an uneasy ride. His mind troubled, Gruffudd was not afraid of battle, injury, or even death. What worried him was the thought that his decision was wrong. Had he made the right choice – had he led his men, the most faithful of his men, to certain death? And his kingdom, Gwynedd, left to the Normans, defenceless? More than anything, he was afraid once again of failing as a leader. Doubts flooded his mind, and because he was on his way to meet the Normans, every argument against such a journey was reinforced. He blamed himself for letting the brothers unsettle him, their visit prompting his decision. No, he was stronger than that, he was his own man, strong-willed, resolute . . . but he kept coming back to his own accusation. Why did he feel such hatred towards Máire's brothers – was it his conscience? No, it was Olaf's manner. He had showed him, the king, nothing but contempt.

'Don't let him trouble you, Gruffudd.' Collwyn looked straight ahead. 'I bet he wishes he was still in Aberffraw.'

He shouldn't let his feelings show. Gruffudd knew that his unease was evident. But this was Collwyn; he could hide nothing from his friend.

'He won't trouble me if he keeps his mouth shut. Keep him away from me, Collwyn,'

'I will.'

They rounded a bend in the path, and looked up towards the summit. There, waiting, were Meirion Goch and Cynwrig Hir, and with them three knights in full armour.

'These are the knights of Hugh, Earl of Chester,' said Meirion Goch. 'They will accompany us, and lead the way.'

Gruffudd moved nearer one of the knights, the one who stood a little apart from the other two.

'Do you understand Welsh?' The knight stared at him.

Gruffudd turned to Latin. 'Do you understand me now?'

'Yes, my lord.'

'Where will I meet the barons?'

'On open land, near the river.'

Again, the same question – 'Who will be there? Which barons?'

'My lord – Hugh, Earl of Chester, will be there to feast with you, and Roger of Shrewsbury.'

'And how many soldiers?'

The man hesitated, 'I . . . I don't know, sir . . . not enough to fight.' He turned to another of the knights, a short man. 'He can speak your tongue, sir . . .'

Gruffudd stared at the other knight, his face hidden by a thick black beard. 'Come nearer,' he commanded. The man led his horse forward. 'Do you serve these men?'

'These men?'

'The Normans,' said Gruffudd impatiently.

'I have no choice in the matter, my lord king.'

'So? Who are you?'

'Tudur ab Idwal, of Tegeingl.'

'Tegeingl . . .' Gruffudd thought instantly of Angharad, he longed to ask him about her. 'Then you must know Robert of Rhuddlan?' Had the face half hidden by the black beard hesitated?

'I know him sir, but not well.'

'But you are well enough acquainted with him to know if he is waiting for me in Rhug?' The same irksome question.

'He is not there my lord.' The reply was certain. Was it too certain?

Gruffudd smiled. 'Tell me . . . as a Welshman,' he lowered his voice. 'Will this meeting benefit me . . . and Gwynedd?'

'It will be of great advantage, sir.' Another firm answer. 'The Normans, they are reasonable people.'

Irritated, Gruffudd thought of Angharad's family. Had everyone in Tegeingl been forced to acquire the same outlook, taught almost like a psalm? *The Normans are just and fair*. He kept his smile fixed. 'Let's go on then. You will stay by my side; I want to hear about Tegeingl . . . and if it is the Norman's intent to attack, then it will be your ribs feeling the blade of my sword!'

The knight stared at Gruffudd, and seeing the fixed smile, he forced his face into a grimace.

They followed the path over the summit and descended steadily through the wooded hill, towards the valley and the river Dee. Once on level ground the path found its way between gorse bushes and thick brambles, the sound of the horse's hooves suddenly alarming a herd of young deer led by an old stag. They disappeared into the golden bushes just missing the hiss of an arrow. Gruffudd once more thought of Angharad, the gold of the gorse bush mirroring the colour of her hair. He turned to Tudur ab Idwal –

'You know Owain ab Edwin of Tegeingl?'

'I know him well, sir.'

'And his children?'

'Yes, I know them.'

'I also know Goronwy and his sister, Angharad.'

'Goronwy and his brother Rhiddid are in Rhug, among the ones that await us.'

Gruffudd showed his surprise, 'Are you certain?'

'Yes sir, I saw them both last night.'

Gruffudd looked at Collwyn, who raised an eyebrow, but kept silent. Somehow Gruffudd felt more at ease. If Angharad and her family from Tegeingl were there, he reasoned, it was unlikely that a trap was waiting for him, given that Owain ab Edwin and his son had just two weeks previously been with him paying their respects. Lightly he asked, 'Is Angharad, their sister, also there?'

The man laughed too loudly, relieved by the change in Gruffudd's mood. 'Oh, no sir! She may be in Rhuddlan castle, but she is not in Rhug. But I know where there are girls, sir . . . noble women and pretty . . . not so far from here . . .'

Gruffudd joined in the banter for a while, but his mind was reeling at the thought of Angharad at Rhuddlan castle. Suddenly his voice lowered again. 'Angharad; she's at the castle, you say. Is she imprisoned there?'

The knight laughed again. 'No, my lord, they say that Robert is . . . very fond of her . . . word has it . . .' But the look on Gruffudd's face stopped his prattle.

'Go on.'

'Well . . . it is rumoured that Robert wishes to make her his wife . . .'

Collwyn, sensing the danger, shouted, 'Smoke!' He pointed towards the river's edge.

Gorse and brambles covered the slopes, reaching the edge of another woodland. The trees formed a semi-circle, leaving a clearing from where the smoke rose in thin, dark columns.

'It's the meeting place,' Tudur ab Idwal said. 'There will be roast oxen, you'll see – you are welcome.'

Gruffudd, still silent, pushed the idea of Angharad at the castle from his mind. He must concentrate on the present. He looked towards the clearing, his eyes taking in the scene – the meeting place, surrounded by a thick cover of trees – an army of a thousand men could easily hide in there. It would be wise to send men ahead, just to check that there were no soldiers. He chose one of his best knights, Cormac, to go ahead, taking fifty men with him. He also ordered the black bearded knight to go with them. They would need an interpreter, and he would need to explain why Cormac and his men had arrived before the king.

Gruffudd ordered his men to dismount and his soldiers to rest. They would wait for the others to return.

By the time they came back, it was almost midday. Cormac came directly to Gruffudd. 'It's a huge area, sir; the forest is far wider than it seems, but we scoured it, and found no Normans, or Welsh.'

'And the meeting point – how many soldiers?'

'Four or five hundred, my lord,' the Irishman smiled, adding, 'No match!'

'Did you see the barons?'

'Yes – two important-looking noblemen, perched on a platform. It appears that they will feed us well.' His voice suddenly became serious. 'Everything looks innocent enough, my lord . . .'

Gruffudd scanned the man's face. He trusted Cormac; he had faith in his judgement.

'Is it your best belief, Cormac?'

'It is, sir.'

Gruffudd gathered his knights, giving his orders in Irish and adding a few words so that the Danes would understand.

'This is my final command – don't be fooled into friendship, be vigilant at all times, keep your weapons at hand. Stay together, don't wander off, we will remain close. Don't let down your guard, and be wary of their drink . . .' A few sniggered, but Gruffudd interrupted, and went on: 'Listen! Look out for any sign, and if you see anything suspicious, come and tell me, Collwyn or Sitriuc immediately. Now get your men ready – make sure they receive all my commands. We will meet them.'

The knights moved on, leaving Gruffudd and Collwyn. Olaf approached. 'What a speech! I'm surprised you think the Irish soldiers needed such plain orders.'

'I'll add another for your benefit. Make sure you relay them to your brothers – you need to follow the same orders as the rest of my men.' Gruffudd turned his horse swiftly, calling to Collwyn, 'Tell the leaders to proceed.'

Soon the company was moving on once more, down the slope and through the gorse bushes, the horses' hooves and the feet of the soldiers trampling the ground, a cloud of dusty earth trailing. It was a clear morning, the weapons gleamed, and the silver bridle of the proud chestnut stallion reflected the dancing rays of the mid-day sun.

5

The wide meadow, the meeting point, lay on the bank of the river Dee. Rising above the meadow was the wooded slope. Near the river a platform had been raised, and on it a table was set. Scattered around the platform were several other heavy tables on trestles. At the raised table, with their backs to the woods, sat Gruffudd, flanked by his men, Collwyn, Sitriuc and Cormac. Cynwrig Hir also sat on the same side, as did the three brothers. Facing them, with their backs to the river, sat the barons – Hugh of Chester and Roger of Shrewsbury, with six of their officers, Meirion Goch and Tudur ab Idwal among them.

Below, the knights were seated, Gruffudd's men along with the Norman knights, and a few Welsh lords whose lands were under Norman rule. Gruffudd recognised Goronwy, Angharad's brother, seated at a table near the platform, with another man he had not met. Gruffudd guessed that this was Rhiddid, the brother. They were very alike – the same watery blue eyes. Goronwy nodded and smiled, but didn't get up to greet Gruffudd.

Further afield, the foot soldiers rested on the grass near the river, scattered in small groups, Gruffudd noted how his men were not far apart, with the baron's men gathered nearer the woods. He also noted that none of the men had settled on the narrow strip of land between the tables and the river.

They had feasted well on roast meat, bread, an array of sweets and fruit, mead and new wines: Gruffudd and his men drinking the mead, but refusing the wine – the Normans drinking only the wine. The sound of feasting increased, the meadow a steady hum of men enjoying a brief respite. At the raised table, a babble of voices – five languages mingled – Welsh, the barons and their officers conversing in French, issuing commands in English to their servants, and then Sitriuc and Cormac slipping easily between Irish and the Danes' tongue.

It all seemed civil enough, as Gruffudd considered the scene; friendly even. He did not, however, trust the two baron. Roger had a ready smile that hid his true feelings. Then there was Hugh – it was difficult to get any true measure of the nature of the Earl of Chester – the man was enormous, the weight of him tended to hide any other impression. His body shook and quivered with any movement, or laughter. The large pale fingers, reaching for the food, seemed soft, shapeless, almost devoid of structure. The baron dipped and washed his fingers carefully in the wooden bowl by his side. His clean-shaven face was devoid of colour, the skin pale and unhealthy, the fleshy face squeezing the eyes into narrow slits, his mouth just a line.

Hugh had spoken only once, to greet him, his voice thin. Roger had spoken little more. Then as they finished eating, Hugh turned to Gruffudd and addressed him in French. Gruffudd replied using the Danes' tongue.

'Do you understand my language?'

Hugh turned to Roger, then he asked Gruffudd, 'Were you ever taught Latin?'

'Certainly,' Gruffudd replied in Latin, the language he had spoken for several years as a boy at school in Sord-Choluim-Cille. Did the Normans think it was only they who were educated?

'Good, good!' Hugh bellowed, as if he were congratulating a young child, who had surprised him with some trick. 'Then we shall speak Latin.' He watched Gruffudd, a smile playing on his thin lips. 'You are an interesting man, Gruffudd ap Cynan.'

'What?' Gruffudd's voice rose. He was piqued by the word 'man'.

The baron held on to his smile. 'Firstly, you are not a true Welshman . . .'

'My father was a true Welshman,' Gruffudd replied. 'Every king, baron, and every man takes his lineage from his father.'

'But you depend heavily on your mother's people.'

Gruffudd watched the eyes almost disappear, this huge man and his shapeless face.

'And you depend on . . .whose family?'

The rolls of fat began to quiver again, the man laughing silently.

Then Roger spoke – slowly, he didn't seem confident in his use of Latin – 'Trahaearn ap Caradog was different. He could depend on the men of Powys for support. It took two armies to defeat him.'

His words touched a raw nerve. Gruffudd felt the anger rising in him; the accusation wasn't entirely true. He had relied on Rhys ap Tewdwr's support on Mynydd Carn, but he alone had led the two armies and ultimately defeated Trahaearn. The assertion had stung. Was the mood among the company changing? Was it their plan to rile him, to anger him so that they had an excuse to attack? He glanced over at his men – everything seemed peaceful enough.

Hugh, serious, went on, 'You asked me, Gruffudd ap Cynan, if I relied on family – well, yes. I rely on any family who is willing to give me their support: that benefits both my cause, and theirs.' He turned to Roger, and continued their conversation in French.

Given the opportunity to take in Hugh's words, Gruffudd had time to think again. They may not be looking for a quarrel after all. Was the purpose of the conference at last coming to a head? Was he about to be given an opportunity to live peacefully as the King of Gwynedd, under their authority, and on the understanding that he would be ready to aid and support, whatever that meant? It could mean of course that he would lead them to plunder Powys, as Trahaearn had done to Gwynedd. Well – he would be willing to comply with their demands – he would then have time to gather a strong army to back him. With a strong army, he could challenge all three – Hugh, Roger and Robert.

Collwyn bent his head towards him. 'What would happen if we asked both Angharad's brothers to join us at our table? They could meet Máire's brothers . . .' he joked, but realised that Gruffudd was unsmiling. 'What is it? Is there something wrong?'

'No, no, I was just . . . well just something the barons said . . .'

'All seems to be well?'

'Earlier, it seemed that they were goading ... provoking, looking for a disagreement. But now . . . I don't know . . . I believe they are about to give me an offer . . .'

'My lord king.' It was Cormac, moving nearer.

'Yes, Cormac?'

'Forgive me, my lord, but you asked us to report any fears . . . anything ... suspicious,' he whispered.

'Well?'

'It might be nothing,' he hesitated, 'but, our backs are to the meadow, and our knights are the same, look, at the other tables.'

Gruffudd took in the scene, Cormac was right. Was it just some officer's doing – simply making the table arrangements easier?

'It might be nothing . . .'

'And there are only Normans on the tables at each end.'

Gruffudd scanned the long line of tables, arranged to the right and left of the platform.

'Yes, I can see your concern, but I don't think it should worry us,' Gruffudd smiled. 'But keep an eye out for the foot soldiers, Cormac.'

'Any concerns?' Roger watched as Cormac returned to his seat.

'None, but naturally my men will come and discuss matters with their king every now and then.'

Gruffudd felt the explanation was needed, although it did sound a rather feeble one. Cormac or any of his other officers might come to his side at any time, if they thought something to be suspicious.

‘I understand.’ Roger looked at Hugh, waiting for a response, but Hugh was watching the men opposite, he studied each one in turn, before returning his gaze to Gruffudd.

‘Gruffudd ap Cynan, I was explaining how I sometimes lean heavily on certain people, and how that is to their advantage.’

‘Yes, go on.’

‘No, you go on . . .’

The King of Gwynedd was not submitting to any baron. Gruffudd smiled – ‘Hugh, Earl of Chester, please go on . . . explain to me what your words mean . . . this *help*, which you refer to . . .?

Hugh gazed uneasily, then he smiled. ‘You could help me serve the king more . . . efficiently . . .’ he tried.

‘King? Which king?’ Gruffudd knew the question would irritate the baron, and that gave him satisfaction.

The narrow eyes flashed again. ‘*The* king of course – William, King of Normandy!’

‘Ah! You must forgive me my lord, but he’s not Gwynedd’s king.’

Hugh, irritated, was about to form another attack when Roger placed a hand on his arm and whispered something in French. He considered Roger’s words and then turned to Gruffudd again, his words less petulant. ‘Yes, I understand your view, and that of the people of Gwynedd, but would it not be wise if they . . . and their king, showed respect to a stronger monarch?’

‘A king with a larger *kingdom*?’

The baron smiled before replying. 'Yes, if you prefer to put it that way.'

Gruffudd paused, choosing his words. 'I show respect to all kings, especially so if they rule a mighty kingdom.'

'Good,' said Roger.

'And your respect towards William's greatest barons?' Hugh added. 'Barons who are superior even to the King of Gwynedd himself?' The word *superior*, deliberately chosen to pique. His words hit hard, and Gruffudd once more felt the anger rising. 'I am not aware of any baron that can usurp the rights of the *King* of Gwynedd.'

A thin laugh escaped, and the huge baron's chest seemed to quiver. 'You are extremely bold, Gruffudd ap Cynan . . . young . . . and amusing.' His breath came heavily, and he spoke softly now. 'And how much respect will you show barons that rule a far larger area than the kingdom of Gwynedd – far greater?'

'I have shown them respect by coming here to meet them.'

'Enough respect also,' Hugh fixed his eyes on the young king, 'to agree to our terms?'

'What terms?'

'We offer you peace, so that you may govern Gwynedd – for a price.'

'The price?'

'A certain amount of tax . . .'

'Yes?'

'Robert of Rhuddlan . . . he would have land in Gwynedd to build his castle . . .'

'No!' Gruffudd replied. 'Do you take me for a fool?'

Hugh ignored the outburst and continued, unperturbed –

'. . . and half of your men to serve us or to serve King William if needed.'

'No! My army stays at my service, mine alone, all of them!' Gruffudd struggled to contain his anger. 'Your terms must come at a smaller prize if peace is to hold.'

'You will very likely pay a far greater price if you refuse,' Hugh sneered.

'Don't decide in haste, Gruffudd ap Cynan,' added Roger.

'You ask too high a price.' Gruffudd glared at the two barons.

Hugh leant his vast frame across the table towards him. 'I cannot understand your unreasonable objection to Robert's wishes. Are you not old friends? His castle would make your load so much lighter . . .'

'He will not enter Gwynedd.'

'Would you object if Hugh, Earl of Chester was to build a castle there?' Roger probed.

'Of course! My kingdom is closed – I will have no Norman castle casting a shadow over Gwynedd.'

The barons glanced at each other. Gruffudd was aware that Collwyn was looking in his direction, but he kept his eyes on the Normans.

Was his response too spirited? Had he been too adamant in his objection? Could he bide time – agree to consider the possibility, and come back with an answer in six months or so – anything rather than rile these two mighty barons now? His stubbornness refused to let him soften his reaction, make things easier for himself – even if it only meant giving them a false answer.

'Our other request . . . regarding half of your army . . . well all your men are here today . . .' Hugh continued to lean forward, his great bulk facing Gruffudd.

'Some of my men are here today,' answered Gruffudd.

'Most of your men . . . I know.'

'Very well, most of my men are present. What difference does that make?'

The sneer was back on the broad face. 'Oh, I think it would be better for you to risk losing just half your men, rather than risk losing all of them.'

So here it was, he had come to this peaceful meeting for this – worse, the conference could be a chance for them to carry out the threat. But a threat would do nothing to abate his will: a threat would only strengthen his resolution – cold water poured onto molten iron. He had to show them that he was fearless. He turned to look at the other tables – his officers drinking, deep in conversation. He cast his eyes over the men there on the meadow; most had finished their feasting, and were just drinking, most resting on the grass. He noted how the baron's soldiers were on their feet. No more than that; there was nothing to make him uneasy. He faced the two barons again.

'Lose all of them?' he turned to Hugh. 'You are the jester now. Your threat does not alarm me, you should realise – I am not a mere nobleman of Edeyrnion or Tegeingl,' he turned towards Roger, 'nor am I Trahaearn ap Caradog! The Normans pose no threat to me . . .' Suddenly his voice rose again, fired by the uncertainty he glimpsed in the men facing him. He raised his empty wooden cup, and brought it down with a crash onto the table, '. . . and their threats do nothing but enrage me further.'

With that, Gruffudd stood up and called out in Irish – 'Get to your feet – we are leaving!' Collwyn, Sitriuc and Cormac rushed to their feet, but Máire's brothers remained seated. 'Get up!' Suddenly he felt a hand on his arm.

'It was clearly a mistake – to threaten you,' Hugh smiled uneasily.

'We were testing you,' added Roger.

'Please stay.' The soft fingers loosened their grip. 'Evidently we must alter the proposals.'

Gruffudd stepped away from the table, 'Your demands?'

'Let us discuss . . .'

Gruffudd paused. Had he done enough? Did they fear him? Would they lessen their demands of him? He ordered his men to sit down again, noting angrily that the three brothers had not moved from their seats.

'Very well, let's hear your new proposals.' Gruffudd took his place again on the bench.

'First,' Hugh smiled broadly, 'in order to regain our earlier good nature, let's enjoy some entertainment, something Roger and myself thought fitting . . .'

'Come, let's drink – mead?' Roger asked.

'Not for me,' replied Gruffudd.

'We have set some competitions – between my men and the men of Chester.'

Hugh interrupted – 'Perhaps your men could compete against the winners?' His voice sweet. 'In jest, of course.'

The change in Hugh's mood was palpable. Was it intentional, a ploy to calm Gruffudd, to appease him? One thing was certain – they wanted to keep him there. The idea of the fearless Irish soldiers competing against the Normans pleased him – they had nothing to fear. 'My men are always ready for a fair challenge!'

'Good!' Hugh washed his fingers in the wooden bowl once more, a servant rushed to his side with a towel, and he dried each of his fat fingers carefully, before getting to his feet. 'Excuse us, we will return to our knights, we need to make sure that the competitors are ready.'

Roger washed and dried his fingers, hurriedly, a broad smile on his face. 'You see, Gruffudd ap Cynan, we take these competitions seriously – the men like to win!' He stepped away from the table and added, 'You have a good vantage point here. I suggest that you turn to face the meadow – the servants will take good care of you, and we will return shortly. I look forward to seeing your men in action.'

Gruffudd watched as the two barons went over to their men, Hugh in one direction, Roger the other.

'They've joined their own men at the end tables,' Collwyn noted.

Gruffudd kept silent, turning to face the clearance on the meadow, his back to the table.

'What are you thinking? Are you happy with the way things have gone?' Collwyn asked, also turning towards the clearance.

'With two as devious as these, it's almost impossible to tell, but I think they want to keep me here, and not offend me more.'

'That would be wise.'

'Yes.'

'And Robert hasn't shown his face – a good omen!'

'I think it is.'

Gruffudd watched as three Norman knights joined the foot-soldiers, moving amongst them, then the foot-soldiers got to their feet and divided into two groups, each group joining Hugh or Roger at the each of the end tables.

'They've arranged themselves into two camps,' Collwyn laughed nervously. 'I hope they take their allegiance seriously, so that they come out of it black and blue!'

From amongst Hugh's men a tall man emerged in a green, woollen tunic. He walked into the clearing and stood there waiting, a thick club in his hand. Then from Roger's camp another man emerged also holding a club and wearing a woollen tunic, of blue hue. Immediately the two men began fighting, clubs raining down on flesh and bone – the two camps yelling their support. Gruffudd's men gathered closer, moving together.

The place erupted into wild yells and with every thud the crowd roared. Sitriuc leapt to his feet, his voice heard above all others. Then Roger's man drew his club down with a heavy blow on the other's head. He staggered, stunned, but stayed on his feet.

'Collwyn, have we anyone that can compete with these two?' asked Gruffudd.

Collwyn hesitated. 'There is one young lad, he's very good – a Dane, but under pressure he can't . . .'

'No! A safer bet.'

'One of Cormac's young officers can outwit most . . . I haven't seen him with a staff but . . .'

Collwyn called Cormac to the table. 'I was about to come to you sir.' Cormac looked at Gruffudd, his face weary.

'And what is your concern this time Cormac?' Gruffudd smiled. 'No – first tell me who this young officer is – can he beat the best of these two?'

'Sir, he could beat both . . . Riagan . . . yes he could beat both men – at the same time!'

Gruffudd, delighted, laughed. 'Excellent!' He had great faith in Cormac's judgment. 'Will you arrange for him to represent me? Now what is it that concerns you Cormac?' Waiting for Cormac's answer, Gruffudd realised that he was the man who would replace Sitriuc one day.

'It's just that the two Welshmen – the red-bearded one and the short, dark one, have both left our table and joined the Earl of Chester.'

Cormac's words left Gruffudd uneasy. Collwyn got to his feet and peered towards the Earl of Chester and there at the table he could see both Meirion Goch and Tudur ab Idwal. 'It won't be as easy to thrust your sword into that one's ribs now if things turn out badly!'

'Cynwrig Hir has remained,' Gruffudd noted. 'As I had guessed, those two have shown their true colours. They couldn't get away fast enough. Cormac, is this a sign?'

'My lord, I cannot tell, it's difficult to know if it's a sign without knowing the pattern. Do the events today follow a pattern?'

'Well – do they?' Gruffudd had expected a clearer answer.

'I've tried to work this out – a clearer pattern might emerge if something occurs on the strip of land that lies between us and the river, the strip of land just behind us here.'

'Something innocent perhaps?' said Gruffudd, beginning to grasp Cormac's reasoning.

'Yes, my lord, the Normans need an excuse, a reason to be there.'

Loud shouts rang out. Gruffudd looked at the competitors; the man in the blue tunic was on the grass, motionless, the other was standing tall, the staff clenched above his head. The crowd applauded, Hugh's men gleefully waving their swords and spears in the air.

'Cormac, tell Riagan that if he can beat the Norman, then I will reward him with the horse I rode when I was in Arfon and Llŷn.'

'My lord, he will defeat him without a reward.'

Gruffudd suddenly felt a surge of anger, and with raised voice he added 'Follow my orders, and hurry!'

'Certainly, my lord.' Cormac hurried away to find Riagan.

'I always find that once I give a man attention or give him standing or prominence, then suddenly he knows better than his king! Cormac has never before questioned any of my orders.'

'He is ambitious . . .' Collwyn realised he had used a new word, and added, 'He longs for you to grant him more authority.'

'Ambitious – yes he is that, and I must try to remember the word. I must be wary that he does not get too arrogant – but not today. Today all I ask of him is his vigilance and cunning.'

Gruffudd's men raised their voices as Riagan in his grey tunic strode forward into the clearing, ready for the fight. He took the club from Roger's man, still on the grass. Riagan turned to face the man standing there in his green tunic.

'And this is Riagan? He's far shorter than his rival.'

No time was wasted. The taller man waving the staff threatened to bring it down heavily on Riagan, but the smaller man danced and side-stepped and avoided the slow, clumsy attack. Then suddenly Riagan stopped, and aimed the club at the other man's stomach, thrusting. The blow brought the big man's head down, bowing almost in front of Riagan. Riagan reached out and struck the man squarely on the nape of his neck. The blow threw the man face down onto the grass.

'Excellent, excellent – a lightning strike!'

All of Gruffudd's men got to their feet, applauding and calling out Riagan's name. Sitriuc, beaming, faced Gruffudd: 'Did you see what he just did? He showed them how it's done!'

'Yes, yes, that gave their pride a blow!'

In the confusion Gruffudd almost lost Collwyn's words: 'Look at what's going on behind us.'

'What is it?' said Gruffudd, still watching the scene on the meadow. Slowly he realised what Collwyn had said, and turned to take in the actions behind him. There, on the narrow strip of land between them and the river, led by a group of two dozen Norman soldiers, were several heavy warhorses. The horses stood in a long line on the bank, drinking, hiding the river from view, and extending away towards the reed bed and the tall rushes beyond.

'The pattern . . . Cormac's words,' Collwyn added slowly. 'Something *is* happening on that strip of land, giving the Normans a perfect excuse to be here . . .'

Gruffudd looked at the long line of horses, their necks bent towards the cool water, their tails whipping away at the flies, and the soldiers just watching.

'Yes,' he said, 'and they seem . . . so harmless.'

6

Two hefty Normans were wrestling on the clearance, when Cormac returned.

'Riagan – what an excellent choice!' Gruffudd nodded.

'As I said.' Cormac beamed with pride.

'He has earned the horse.'

'Yes, my lord – if you say so.'

Then Gruffudd changed the tone of his voice. 'Look at the river.'

The pride evident on his face, Cormac nodded, 'Yes, I expected this.'

'Why? Would you care to explain?' Gruffudd kept his voice steady, he did not want Cormac to think that he relied too heavily on his findings.

'Well, my lord, just think . . .'

'So, you give out the orders now . . .?' It was not his intention to confront Cormac today.

The officer, surprised, replied, 'Oh no, my lord, I was merely trying to point out . . .'

'Then choose your words wisely,' Gruffudd said curtly.

Cormac glanced at Collwyn before continuing. 'I have noticed . . . I believe that your position and that of your officers . . . Well, we are positioned in a narrow line – the Norman soldiers on one side, they have moved and are now placed in front of the tables, the Norman officers have gathered in front of those tables there, and behind them more soldiers have appeared between the tables and the river. My lord, we are surrounded . . .'

Collwyn interrupted, speaking in Irish. 'And if things get out of hand the barons have retreated to the tables set behind their officers, where it will be easy to defend them. And Meirion Goch and Tudur ap Idwal are with them.'

Gruffudd surveyed the scene. Norman foot soldiers were now sitting on the grass in front of the tables. They had spread and formed an almost solid line from one set of tables to the other – leaving only a narrow passage opposite where Gruffudd stood on the platform. He noticed that there were now at least two Norman rows of men between himself and his own soldiers. He spoke slowly, 'What you suspect might be correct . . . and yet they may be innocent moves . . .' He looked over his shoulder. 'There are only a couple of dozen behind us – not enough to be a threat . . .'

'What if there are more, my lord . . .'

'I haven't finished!' Gruffudd glared. 'Of course, there may be dozens more . . . the rushes over there, they could lay hidden . . .'

Loud roars came from the onlookers, as one of the wrestlers fell heavily to the ground, the winner beaming.

'Another of Hugh's men,' said Collwyn.

'Have we someone who can beat him?' asked Gruffudd, his enthusiasm gone.

'Sitriuc's brother – I saw him throw a bull once.'

'Yes, I seem to remember, go and find him, Collwyn.'

Collwyn went to find Sitriuc's brother. Then Gruffudd turned to Cormac, 'Take a few of the soldiers with you, move some of our horses to the river and take a good look at what's going on there.'

Cormac strode off, glad of the chance to serve. Gruffudd stared again at the horses, they had finished drinking, moving their heads impatiently, waiting; held there in a tight row along the bank. Why? Collwyn returned.

'He expected to be called – Sitriuc's brother.'

'Good.' Indifferent.

'What is it?'

Gruffudd faced his friend. Collwyn may not have the quick wit of Cormac, but he could hide nothing from him. Collwyn was the one who understood him, knew of all his doubts and strengths, understood him better than even his own mother had done. Collwyn had served him, better than any brother. Having Collwyn was like having a copy of himself, except that he was always the leader . . .

Gruffudd's men applauded as Sitriuc's brother took his place in the clearance, a short man, solid, his bare arms ready.

'The horses on the bank, they've been there now for some time, it can't be good . . .'

'Most of our horses are back under those trees,' said Collwyn.

They watched as Cormac and three officers went over to the foot soldiers. Fifteen of them got to their feet and followed Cormac towards their horses still underneath a canopy of trees. The excited roar of the crowd in anticipation, the two wrestlers now facing each other . . . Cormac and his men spreading out in a row as they approached the horses . . . Cormac leaving the line . . . approaching the woods alone . . . Collwyn's voice,

'Something's wrong! Cormac's leaving the others. A horse perhaps . . . in those brambles . . .'

Cormac disappeared from view . . . then re-appeared starting across the meadow, slowly at first, then his step quickening . . . Collwyn's voice again, laughing,

'Here he comes – he's seen something, I suppose!'

Another deafening roar from the crowd. Gruffudd watched as the Norman was held across the broad shoulders of the other wrestler . . . Sitriuc yelling, 'Sir, watch my brother raise him even higher . . .'

Then Collwyn's voice – 'Look, even Cormac is dancing with delight!'

Gruffudd saw Cormac moving unsteadily . . . Gruffudd thought how strange his movements were, his hands raised across his face like that . . . Cormac stopping, then swaying . . . before falling onto his face on the grass . . . The crowd roaring . . . Sitriuc's voice . . .

'My brother, he's got him . . . round he goes – throw him!'

Gruffudd stared at Cormac, still lying there – the Irishman on the ground, his head and arms jerking, before becoming still . . . And Gruffudd seeing the arrow, its tip buried in Cormac's neck . . . the voice of Sitriuc – 'One, two, three . . . throw him!'

Gruffudd on his feet – 'Cormac! He's been hit!' His voice lost in the roaring of the crowd.

Collwyn shouting. 'The Norman – his back is broken, he won't get up again!'

The yelling intensifying, Gruffudd clutching at Collwyn's arm. 'Look – Cormac! An arrow in his neck!'

'Cormac!' Collwyn, his voice a scream. 'How? Who?'

'I don't know! Go to him, Collwyn, bring him here. Tell the ones who went with him to carry him back here. See if they saw anything! Go!'

Gruffudd having to yell to make himself heard above the confusion.

Collwyn jumps . . . runs . . . through the foot soldiers . . . Gruffudd watches . . . Collwyn gets within ten yards of where Sitriuc's brother is standing – victorious, but runs on . . . reaches Cormac . . . kneels by his side, cradles Cormac's head... Arrows rain from the direction of the woods, raining down on both men . . . Gruffudd watches, horrified, as Collwyn, three arrows embedded in his back, turns and starts to haul Cormac's body . . . before collapsing in a heap beside the Irishman. Gruffudd takes out his sword and shouts for his officers to join the foot soldiers on the meadow. A horn sounds from the direction of the woods, another horn answers from Hugh's table. Then a long row of archers appears, stepping steadily out of the darkness of the trees, each arrow pointing at Gruffudd and his men. Gruffudd shouts – '*Brad! Brad!* Treachery!' Fear grips him, the same terrible fear that gripped him at the battle of Bron-yr-erw, when the men of Llŷn and Eifionydd turned their backs on him, his situation hopeless. But then he had managed to flee from Bron-yr-erw . . . he had reached the Menai . . . He could go for the river now – breaking through the row of knights standing beyond the tables, he could make it to the river, seize their horses and get away, his officers and himself, and disappear . . . he would find freedom in Eryri . . . Menai . . . But what of his soldiers, three hundred of his best men . . . Collwyn – he might be alive . . . But he was King of Gwynedd . . . the river his only chance. The sound of more horns beyond the river. Another army appears beyond the row of knights, another company of soldiers, a throng of horses and a forest of spears! Reaching the river is impossible. The sound of his voice calling out to his men 'Get to the meadow – join the foot soldiers!' . . . His voice a scream, 'Follow me!'

He ran, sword in hand, thrashing out and through the enemy line – across the meadow rallying his men. A blast, again from the edge of the woods, another from the same direction, yet another call from the edge of the river, echoed by another from one of the tables.

Then suddenly – silence. In the strange silence that followed, Hugh's reedy voice called out in Latin – 'Gruffudd ap Cynan! Gruffudd ap Cynan! Hear me!'

Gruffudd, rage spurring him forward, said nothing.

'Gruffudd ap Cynan! Listen to me! You have a choice . . .'

Gruffudd stopped and looked for the baron, hidden behind his officers. He looked around and realised that only a handful of his own knights had been able to follow. How had the situation changed so rapidly? Everyone had been gripped, watching the wrestlers grapple. They had been tricked – no one had noticed the events taking place by the river. And because of the yelling and uproar following the match – only a few of his officers had heard his orders. Now, the screech of the horn had silenced the crowd, and he could feel the silence on his skin like a cold sweat . . . No one moved, all waiting for his response. What choice did he have other than to live or die?

'Gruffudd ap Cynan – you have a choice – surrender yourself and become my prisoner, and all your men will be spared, they can return to their homes . . .' Only silence, a strange and terrible sadness gripped Gruffudd. 'Or refuse to surrender and choose to fight – there will only be one outcome if that is your choice – look around you, Gruffudd ap Cynan – you, along with all of your men, will be slaughtered,' screeched the thin voice. 'Each and every one of you – no one will be spared. Make your choice!'

Two rows of archers stood at the edge of the trees, and on the riverbank stood two rows of soldiers, spears gleaming.

Dread and horror slowly shrouded his thoughts. Out of habit, Gruffudd turned to look for his old friend Collwyn, for advice. Remembering, he walked slowly to where Collwyn lay, stretched alongside Cormac, the three arrows in his shoulder like three vulgar flowers, blood forming dark pools underneath his woollen tunic. Cormac stared ahead, his lips moving but no words forming, but Collwyn's eyes were closed. 'Collwyn!'

Gruffudd kneeled, and lowered his head towards his friend. 'Collwyn!'

The eyes opened.

'Will you live?'

The eyes stared, and Gruffudd gripped his arm. 'Did you hear the demon's words? His offer?' He lowered his face so that he could almost touch Collwyn. 'What should I do, Collwyn?'

A faint smile appeared on Collwyn's face. 'I can't move . . .'

Gruffudd held Collwyn's face between his hands. 'But you want to live?'

The same smile, and the answer, barely audible. 'Do you want to live, Gruffudd . . .?'

Gruffudd got to his feet, straightened, but his voice was breaking. 'You fool, everything is lost!'

The sound of feet rushing towards him, Sitriuc holding his huge sword held high – 'My lord, choose to fight! They fear us!'

Gruffudd stared at the mighty officer, unable to say a word. Sitriuc stepped away from his king, but continued to brandish his sword. He shouted to his fellow officers, then came the hissing sound of arrows. Sitriuc groaned and fell to his knees, six arrow-heads in his flesh. Then Collwyn's dry, rasping voice – 'Choose life, Gruffudd!'

'Hurry up, Gruffudd, make your decision, before all of you are slain.' Hugh's voice shouting, as a group of his foot soldiers gathered around Gruffudd.

'Your word – is there any integrity in a promise made by a devious devil like you?'

Hugh replied, 'None of your men, apart from the three who were about to spoil our plans, have been injured . . .' then gave a screech of laughter. 'Don't you realise, Gruffudd ap Cynan, that we have a thousand men ready to attack if word is given? Six hundred arrows pointing directly at you and your men. I have given no sign that they should commence – yet.'

With the baron's words, the soldiers fell silent, every eye on Gruffudd. He took a few paces towards where he guessed Hugh was hidden. He stopped, and turning to his friend, there by his feet, said to him, 'You must live . . . listen to me – don't give up!' Then he turned to his soldiers adding in Irish, 'Don't let him die, do your best for him and for Cormac and Sitriuc . . .' Sitriuc's brother cradled the giant's head. 'Take the three of them home, alive or otherwise, you must not leave them here . . .' His voice faltered.

Then he walked towards the furthest table, pushing his sword into its scabbard. Hugh emerged from behind his officers, accompanied by Meirion Goch. A sudden rage flashed through Gruffudd, an urge to take his sword out again, but he knew it was hopeless. Suddenly the sound of heavy warhorses broke the silence. Gruffudd turned his head, stupidly hoping that some phantom Welsh army had emerged from over the hill to save him. From between the ranks of archers a company of knights appeared. Their helmets with the nose guard, the chain mail and the shield, with its curved top and pointed end, all proved that more of the enemy had arrived. Gruffudd looked at the leader. The man had a short, dark beard, his helmet and shield were also black, and he sat straight-backed in the saddle. As if struck by a spear, Gruffudd knew. Instinctively, his hand went for his sword, but before he could move, four officers got hold of him, his arms stilled.

Again it was Hugh's reedy voice: 'It's too late for that, Gruffudd ap Cynan!' – a scornful laugh – 'It would be foolish to give Robert of Rhuddlan an excuse to slay you here in front of your own men.'

7

He leaned against the side of the dungeon, the darkness reflecting his desolation. His fear was overtaken by despair, and the realisation that he had failed once more. If only he was held captive in Wales, Rhuddlan even, then he would stand a chance of being saved.

When he'd been dragged in chains across the river to the manor house, he'd held on to the hope that an army, led perhaps by Gwyncu, would appear – the men of Gwynedd joining the Danes and Irish in a bid to free him. Even when flanked by a hundred or so of the Norman soldiers and knights, in the first light of dawn on the following day, he had held on to the hope of seeing an army of his men appearing over the summit of the Berwyn, descending into the valley below. No one appeared. When he grasped that their intention was to follow the river to Chester, he knew it was foolish to hang on to the hope of being saved. By late afternoon they had reached Chester, and seeing the tall, red walls surrounding the castle, perched on a hill, affirmed his fears. And when he was thrown into the dungeon beneath one of the castle's towers, his despair was complete.

He had been there for days – all alone, without food, and the only water he found was a dirty pool by some stones in the wall. No one had spoken to him on their journey to

Chester – neither Hugh or Roger had approached him when they had been at the manor house at Rhug. At the time of Gruffudd's capture Robert had spat, 'This time, Gruffudd ap Cynan, you have failed utterly!'

Someone was walking on the wooden boards above the vault. Gruffudd listened. The footsteps were heavy . . . Hugh perhaps? They paused near the opening to the vault, but just out of sight. Was he to be lifted from the pit, was he going to be fed or given water? His thirst terrible, he wanted to call for water, but stopped – he would not beg. Then a torch was held up. Gruffudd straightened, taking in his surroundings. He was in a rounded pit, dug from the reddish rock, and he noticed a trickle of water shone in the light, just above his head, but not out of reach.

Above him, two voices laughed, then the light disappeared and the feet moved away again. Gruffudd reached out for the trickle of water, guessing the direction – damp soil, the sharp rock, then a coolness on his finger-tips. It was too high for him to reach with his mouth, so he reached out with his fingers and rubbed his damp fingers onto his cracked lips. Then he found a small cleft in the rock where the water formed droplets – he collected them onto his fingers, and his thirst eased a little. As his fingers touched the rock, Gruffudd knew that several other fingers had touched the same surface in desperate times.

He sat directly below the cleft, so that he could find the exact spot again in the darkness. He tried to spit the taste of dirt from his mouth, but his mouth was dry. He stared in the direction from where the light had come, looking for a pale sliver that would tell him if it was daylight. The darkness fed his misery, he could feel himself sway, the weakness taking its toll, a sharp edge of rock pressing into his skin. He thought again of Collwyn – the arrows in his back. Was he alive? What had become of his other soldiers? Tears stung, not of longing for his men, but tears of hopelessness at the acknowledgement of his devastating failure. He would have to shut Collwyn and his soldiers – and Angharad – from his thoughts. He could not bear thinking of his loss. He lay down on the floor, becoming aware once more of the pain in his hands – the irons tight at his wrists, pain throbbing in tune with the thud of his heart. Slowly he managed to nudge the shackle further towards his hand, easing the pain a little. He listened, hoping to hear anything – voices, footsteps, the wind, mice even. There were no mice, there was no food . . . Had his predecessors been starved to death, their fingers reaching for the drops on the rock before fading into nothingness? Was this his fate? He remembered how he had once seen slaves on the island of Saltee, emaciated, and left there to die: some of them having bitten parts of their limbs, their left arms . . . He moved his legs in a circular motion, looking for remains, bones. The chain constraining his legs hitting small stones but no remains . . . The Normans would have lifted the bodies from the pit, they would have raised the prisoners from this hell before they starved. But not before the brutality of the place had destroyed their resolve – their spirit broken.

Was this his fate? Suddenly his innate stubbornness rose in him once more. He would survive the pit, if only he was allowed to live and eat. If he was allowed to live, his body resilient, his spirit tenacious – he could survive anything.

A further six or seven days passed, his determination weakening. If only he could eat! The pain in his body bit into his resolve. Then one evening when the two men shone the torch once more into the dungeon, he struggled to his feet. The words formed in his mouth, the words begging for food, but again his will stood fast, he would not beg. The two men moved away, their voices receding, leaving only their sneers echoing around his prison.

So many days dragged on, the pain in his stomach easing only when he lay on the floor, his knees pulled up, his fist pushed into the pit of his stomach. Often, he would reel, and fall over, trying to find the dampness on the rock, at other times he would only be faintly aware that the torch was back, and the sound of harsh laughter, louder, but further away. He could not get up.

Once, when the pain receded a little, he slept. He awoke to hear his own voice calling for Collwyn; his tongue swollen, his lips cracked and sore. He had to get up, he had to find the dampness in the rock – he had failed too often lately, his strength waning, he could not stay on his feet. He got up and leaned against the side of his prison. Raising his arms was an effort; he tried again and failed, the shackles heavy, his arms weak. He fell to his knees, scraping the edge of the rock, his fingers collecting the dirt, bits of moss – he put it in his mouth, sipping at the moss, another mouthful, and yet another. Scraping the dirt into his hands tired him. He lay there, the pain in his stomach burning, scorching his entrails. Soon, he knew, he would die. He began to pray, the darkness engulfing him, the dirt forming a crust on his lips . . . the same lips moving . . . praying . . . asking for forgiveness, forgiveness for his weakness, for failing . . . Then the cursing, his voice louder now, cursing Hugh, Robert and Meirion Goch, the others whose names he could not remember . . . Asking blessing for his loved ones, Collwyn, Angharad, Máire . . . Begging for a swift death, not this . . . Pleading for Saint Columba's delivery of his soul.

He repeated the Amen, over and over. He could not find the damp dirt. All he could do was lie there, his knees raised, his thoughts dulled. Sometimes he would repeat the prayer in his mind, but he could never reach the end, wishing he could sink into nothingness – stay there until the end.

In this state of semi-consciousness, he had a faint sensation that he was being shaken, voices echoing. Was it one of the nightmarish thoughts which visited him sometimes? He was being lifted; his name called. Pain, loud shouts in his ears. The dungeon lit, blinding him. When he finally opened his eyes, the black shapes surrounding him swayed. A pale shape formed into a large face, shifting in front of him, a pale moon quivering in a pool of water – shouting now, calling to him in Latin, calling his name.

'Gruffudd ap Cynan – filthy swine!' Voices sneering, 'A king? No! A stinking swine!'

More laughter, shifting, moving away, then nearing again.

'But we must lift you from here, Gruffudd ap Cynan. Get to your feet!'

The face, the dark shapes and the pit sank into darkness.

8

Cold water in his eyes, nose, ears, mouth – choking him, but he couldn't move his face.

Another voice calling out in Latin – 'Drink, Gruffudd ap Cynan, while you have the chance.'

His head raised slightly from the water, he half opened his eyes. It was daylight, and his head was being held in a barrel of water. Gasping, he drank deeply, relief flowing as he felt the cool stream rush through his body. His head was jerked suddenly upwards.

'Not too much now – we don't want you spewing in front of the earl!'

Jeering again – 'Show a bit of respect – you need to get washed, the earl will not host a dirty dog.'

His head back in the barrel. In, out, in, out, his face pushed into the water, then raised again, over and over. Someone grabbed his head by the hair – pulling his head up again, the man leaned over him, staring. Slowly Gruffudd could make out the face, his eyes growing accustomed to the light. The man was a Norman knight; the other two who held on to his arms were soldiers. He realised that they were standing inside the castle wall. He recognised his surroundings.

'You look a little more human, I expect you'll live a few more days.' Laughter again. Somehow, Gruffudd felt that he should recognise the voice too, but he could not think why.

'Come on, Hugh the Earl of Chester wants to see you . . .' another sneer, 'for a final meeting.'

Gruffudd was dragged by the two soldiers along the edge of the wooden building, across the yard and up a flight of earthen steps, through the gateway and into the upper bailey. They reached another large building made of wood. The knight entered first, then returned and without uttering a word, pushed Gruffudd in ahead of him.

Gruffudd saw that he was in a long, wide room – the main hall. Tables stood along the length of each side of the hall, leaving a gap down the centre of the room; at the end was another table, at which several men sat. One of them raised his hand, signalling for Gruffudd to be brought forward. The two soldiers took his weight, his legs being too weak to carry him, his head heavy.

'That's near enough, Philip!' Hugh's voice, 'We don't want to be put off our feast now . . .' More mirth. Gruffudd raised his head. Four men sat at the table, Hugh's large frame in pride of place at the centre. At his right hand sat the dark-haired Robert of Rhuddlan. Gruffudd felt a hatred stirring inside him – how he wished he could spew the contents of his stomach over the table.

'Is it not a great sadness,' Hugh's voice feigning sympathy, 'seeing a young king in such a state, does he not rather resemble a filthy slave . . .?' Laughter again, and Hugh waited for the company to settle before continuing, 'But you must realise, your stubbornness and pride got you here. If you had only agreed to let us procure half your army, and if only you had just let my friend here – Robert of Rhuddlan – build a . . . modest castle on your land, then . . .' his fleshy fingers gesticulating, 'you would still be reigning over your . . . small kingdom now . . . safe and secure.' He wiped his mouth on the edge of his blue cloak. Gruffudd's head lolled – the reedy voice went on. 'But your pig-headedness and your pride were far too great, far too great for someone of your stature: you lost everything. Everything! Worst of all . . .'

'The others?' Gruffudd's question struggled to be heard, his voice a weak cry.

'What has the creature to say, Philip?'

'I believe he is asking of his men, sir.' The knight said.

Gruffudd struggled to raise his head again, fixing his eyes on the fat baron.

'Oh! I understand!' Hugh's voice again. Then he turned to Robert, and they both snorted. 'You tell him Robert, as it was your plan.'

Robert of Rhuddlan straightened. Gruffudd's mind cleared. He had to be prepared, he had to be ready to hear of his men's fate.

'Gruffudd ap Cynan . . .' the voice hard, 'it was my plan to get you and your Irishmen to Rhug. You are my prisoner. I was aided of course by my cousin the Earl of Chester, and by my good friend Roger of Shrewsbury. You are in my power. Remember this. Gwynedd is in my power, remember this also.'

Gruffudd raised his head again. 'The others?' he cried.

Robert stared at him, his voice steady but full of arrogance. 'They will never fight for you again . . . or for any other king,' he sneered.

Angry tears stung at Gruffudd's eyes. He reached out as far as he could, and the soldiers gripped him harder. 'You cursed devil – damn you to eternal hell . . . if I could defile this table I would . . .'

The smile vanished. 'If you could, but you are useless, Gruffudd. There is nothing you can do now, Gruffudd ap Cynan, except die.' His voice raised. 'And I will see to it that you will not have to wait long for death!'

Hugh interrupted, 'Tell him the men's fate.'

The two barons glanced at each other, quietly exchanging words in French. Gruffudd noticed a difference in their tone, was there a disagreement? Then again, it made no difference to him. His head sank again.

'Gruffudd ap Cynan – is it your wish to die in the pit?'

Gruffudd did not respond. What did it matter now where he was to die? He could last another three days on the damp pit floor, but that would be the end. Then Robert spoke again.

'Hugh, sir, is it not customary to blind any pirate that is caught and brought to justice? Is this cursed being nothing more than an ambitious pirate?'

That word! Gruffudd's thoughts were again in Aberffraw with Angharad. Then Hugh spoke.

'Call him a pirate if you like, but don't forget that any loot or land a pirate may have, must by law be given over to the king.'

Someone growled – was it Robert? His words were unclear. Gruffudd's stomach burned, and his head spun . . .

'Gruffudd ap Cynan, the pit is the place for taming unruly, stubborn prisoners. Are you tamed?' The thin voice mocking.

'Of course you are, as with all prisoners, you are no different. Although Robert's prisoner, while you are here, you are my responsibility . . .'

'When order is restored in Gwynedd, he will be moved to Rhuddlan,' Robert's voice again, the words a quick, angry stream. 'That will be the end of him.'

Was there a quarrel looming? Gruffudd's head cleared a little, then Hugh's eyes were on him again. 'We are civilised people. It is the tradition within the courts of the *main lords* in Normandy . . .' the weight given to the words *main lords*, made Robert sit up impatiently, '. . . to respect the status of a prisoner. You have very little status – however I will grant you the chance to live. You will not lose your eyes. You deserve that much respect. You will be moved out of the pit and fed . . . half the portion given a slave.'

Hugh watched angrily as Robert gave another sneer. He opened his mouth ready to respond, but thought better of it and turned back to Gruffudd. 'But you must understand – if you make any attempt to escape – you will die.'

Gruffudd felt the ground beneath him give, then Hugh's voice again – 'Is that clear?'

The walls pitched, his stomach churned, and he saw Hugh struggle to his feet, his voice a shrill cry, 'Is that clear? Answer me!'

Gruffudd could see Hugh's vast frame above him through the sweat that ran into his eyes. He knew that Hugh wanted to show his cousin that he had the authority, waiting for the prisoner's word. Gruffudd knew what he had to do, he would not concede, he would not give in, he would not answer, or give his word to this man, he would not bow to any Norman.

'Answer me, serf!'

The shrill voice screamed, the vast pale face blotched red with rage.

Gruffudd kept silent.

'Rip his tongue out!' Robert shouted.

'Bring him here! Philip, drag him to me!'

The knight gave Gruffudd a shove, and he was against the edge of the table, the large face near his, the words came between gasps, as if the man struggled to keep his composure.

'I order the prisoner to answer! Give me your answer!'

They had taken Collwyn, Sitriuc and Cormac from him, they had slaughtered them, and the others, hundreds of his best men, some of whom had been with him on his very first journey, when he had first seen Abermenai. They had taken his kingdom, Gwynedd from him . . . forever! And now they wanted his obedience. His mouth dry, he collected the little moisture he had on his tongue and spat into the face in front of him.

Robert roared, and his cousin screeched. Darkness enveloped Gruffudd as Hugh's fist came down with a thud onto the side of his face.

9

He was alive. Gruffudd opened his eyes. He was in a different place, not in the pit, but on a dusty earthen floor, the place dimly lit. Moving his head, he felt a new pain in the side of his head. Hugh: he recalled the thud. His tongue was still there, leathery and dry. He knew he had another, worse recollection. Slowly the horror of it formed in his memory: his soldiers – all lost. Their names rushed through his head, their faces – his faithful, brave men. A moan escaped him, he began cursing the barons. Suddenly he realised that someone else was in the room. He recalled Hugh's faint promise of food, was it possible?

He tried to turn onto his side so that he could take in his surroundings, but his legs were pinned down. He was in a wooden construction, with light coming in from an opening at one end. His feet, he could see, were manacled, and the chain between each bond was connected to a stout central post. He tried to focus. Someone was standing, leaning on the central post. As Gruffudd struggled to raise himself to a sitting position, the light hit the blade of a sword – the guard, pointing his weapon in his direction. The man left the post and the sword leapt towards Gruffudd's chest. The man leaned forward and placed the sharp edge of his sword on Gruffudd's throat. He wanted to call out, but his voice disappeared. He became aware of a trickle of blood running down the skin of his neck, slowly, delicately, like the touch of an insect. A face loomed above him, dark hair, bearded. His breath reeked of mead.

'Are you afraid, Gruffudd ap Cynan? Ha! You tremble with fear!' A Welsh voice, mocking.

'A Welshman!' Gruffudd gasped, his voice a small scream.

'If I . . .' the man drawled '. . . pushed the point just a little further . . . you would die . . . before I could even tell the baron the . . . sad news.'

Gruffudd could feel the point jutting into his throat, the blood seeping over his skin. He tried to concentrate on the words of a prayer, but his mind was gripped by fear; he couldn't think clearly.

'You are a Welshman!' Meirion Goch forgotten.

'I despise you, Gruffudd ap Cynan! The men that follow you – the evil Danes and Irish! I would give my arm just for the pleasure of sinking this sword further into your throat.'

Gruffudd struggled to move out of this maniac's reach, but the man held firmly on to his hair, forcing the sword's edge further along Gruffudd's throat.

'You're a vindictive bastard!'

Footsteps neared, the sound of a sword against metal, and a French voice from the opening. Gruffudd's head was free from the maniac's grasp. Two men approached. Gruffudd recognized Philip and another of the soldiers who had dragged him into the hall. The knight stood staring down at the prisoner, and turned to the guard.

'Your duty was to watch the pig, not bleed him!' The voice light, almost a banter.

'But what if he was trying to escape?' The man tried in his lame Latin.

Philip took one look at the chain, manacles and hefty post. 'What? He tried to escape?'

The Welshman smiled, 'He . . .was thinking of it!'

'Then you did well – just to give him a small warning.' All three laughed, then the knight stopped abruptly. 'But, don't kill him, not on any account, as pleasurable as it may seem. That honour will not be yours. Understood?'

'It would be my greatest pleasure . . .'

'Understand this, Welshman – if he dies under your watch, then you will take his place in those chains.' The Welshman smiled, and pushed his sword into its scabbard.

'And . . . if you for any reason change your feelings towards this prisoner, and he . . . somehow manages to escape on your watch – you will lose your eyes. Still clear?'

'Help him?' The Welshman laughed. 'Never!'

The knight glanced at Gruffudd. 'No, he will never escape. He can't even get to his feet.' He grabbed hold of Gruffudd's arm. 'It's time to feed him, before it is too late.' He lowered his face towards Gruffudd. 'Gruffudd ap Cynan! Do you hear me?'

Gruffudd stared at him, but did not answer. His only right – to remain silent. As long as he could refuse to answer them, then they had not defeated him. Did the knight understand?

'It was a mistake, spitting at Baron Hugh. You may have worse enemies, but none mightier than him. It would serve you well to remember this.'

Gruffudd closed his eyes. He was aware that the knight

and the soldier had gone. He heard the knight giving the guard an order. Then the Welshman returned.

'Did you hear what he said, Gruffudd? I am not allowed to kill you, but I can have my fun . . . with Gwynedd's king!' The sneer returning, 'Get to your feet, oh mighty King!'

His foot thrust at Gruffudd's ribs. Gruffudd winced, but did not move.

'I'll get you on your feet, and walking . . . Get up, before this sword has another go at your skin. Up, your majesty . . . up.' Another kick. 'You're a stubborn bastard. Get up . . .'

The guard bent over as if to grab hold of the chain between Gruffudd's hands, and yank him to his feet. Gruffudd gathered all his feeble strength and raised his arms suddenly bringing the chain down on the bridge of the guard's nose. The guard jumped back, his nose bloody.

'I'll shred you for this!' he roared.

Two soldiers rushed to the opening. 'What is it?' one shouted in Latin, before snorting, 'You Welsh, you are such great friends!'

'I'll cut him to shreds . . .' The guard took hold of his sword once more.

'Philip needs to see you.' The other soldier barked.

'No, I have to watch the prisoner . . . that's my order.' The guard stood, raging, the blood dripping from his nose.

'Philip is waiting at the watchtower. Hurry up!'

The guard wiped his nose on his sleeve. 'I have to teach this one a lesson first . . .'

'No . . .'

But the sword was in Gruffudd's face before the soldier

could continue. The soldier rushed at the guard, pushing him hard against the wall. He shouted in French, and the second soldier rushed in.

'Are you mad?' he shouted. 'Can't you see, he's half dead as it is! Just one more injury, and he will be a dead prisoner.'

The guard laughed again and pushed the soldier away.

'I hope Philip is amused when he finds out,' said the second soldier. 'If you had ever been trained in a proper army, you would have learnt how to take care of that temper of yours.'

'Philip knows that his prisoner is safe with me . . .' the guard bellowed as he left. 'As safe as a mouse in an owl's beak!'

Gruffudd didn't catch his next words, his mind dull and the pain in his limbs worse now that the immediate danger was over. He lay helpless, eyes closed, his mind in turmoil. Another voice, above him in a strange void, was calling – words linked in a strange, inexplicable stream, just one clear word echoing – 'Death! Death! Death!'

He opened his eyes wide, as the word repeated over and over – but there was no one there. The words stopped and his mind cleared for a moment. He looked at his surroundings. He was alone. The meeting with Hugh came back to him – a vague recollection. Had one of them – Phillip perhaps, said that he would be fed? Or was the promise another one of his dreams – a dream so convincing he thought it must be true – just like the recurring dream he had when in the pit, that he was standing in the rain? Were the soldiers about to return with food and water? Perhaps they had gone – knowing it was too late to save him. Had Philip told the Welshman to leave him alone – not to let him die – then again had he not heard a voice echoing around his prison chanting 'Death! Death!'?

The hunger pains struck again, causing him to double up. A fever raged through his head, his eyes blurring again. He wished he could pass out once more – anything to stop the pain – his mind reeling. His mother telling him to finish his porridge, and if he did so every day, then he would be strong – stronger than his father – he had the blood of the finest Dane in him . . . The sea breeze drifted over him – the sand in his face, in his eyes, nose, in his mouth, coarse grains in his throat . . . choking him . . . he tried to call . . .

Then Angharad appeared – her lips on his, her mouth moist and cool . . . but he wanted to cry out – he could taste the Norman's wine on her lips. The taste filled his mouth, the wine dripping from his mouth, over his chin, sinking into his beard, onto his clothes, his chest. He moved, Angharad moving with him, her arms around him, her voice calling, louder, the voice changing, someone calling – 'Gruffudd ap Cynan . . . Gruffudd ap Cynan . . .'

His eyes wide. 'Angharad!' he gasped, his voice clear.

Two faces stared down at him – the soldiers. A wooden bowl in his hand, one of the soldiers kneeled beside him, water from the bowl dripping down Gruffudd's chin.

'Drink – slowly,' he said.

10

The same two soldiers brought him water or milk half a dozen times over the next three days. Then he was given a bowl of broth and some bread every evening, but no more milk. The pain in his stomach gradually lessened, his mind clearing. He could get up, and a few days after having the broth, he could walk a little. Dragging the chain around the hut, his feet were sore, but he was determined to move again.

During the day he would look forward to his meal, then after eating he wished for darkness and peace so that he could sleep. Nothing else mattered. He saw himself as nothing more than a frail creature tied to a post, waiting all day for a single miserly meal, with nothing to pass the long hours – just waiting for the next bowl.

At one time he had hoped they would add an extra bowl of broth and bread, just enough to strengthen him a little. After several weeks of hoping, he realised that all he could expect was just enough to keep him alive, but not enough to give him any of his former strength. Keeping him weak meant he could never escape.

The pangs in his guts remained, but Gruffudd got used to hunger. The darkness within him, however, he could not get used to. Sometimes the despair paralysed him for hours. Then he would lie still, bent double, tears welling. He knew the tears were a result of his frailness, not of any particular sadness. The sadness, despair and fear became obscure, manifesting as a feeling of absolute despondency. He was to be transferred to Rhuddlan, where Robert would take his revenge – would he be blinded? He was being kept alive just to give the Baron of Rhuddlan the pleasure of finally killing him. Strangely, he did not fear the outcome – it was as if the total despair he felt dulled all other fear.

He endured intense loneliness, made worse by his own stubbornness – he would not talk, he would not co-operate. When the two soldiers had first brought him milk and water, they had tried to converse with him – the one who spoke Latin had spoken to him many times but he would not answer. They were Philip's men, Edric and Richard. Edric spoke Latin – he was the one who had stopped the Welshman's attack, and eventually it was Edric alone who brought Gruffudd his daily ration. He often asked Gruffudd if he felt stronger, then when he understood that Gruffudd would not answer, he left him without uttering a word – leaving the bowl of broth and water by the post, watching Gruffudd eat from a distance.

Every two or three days Philip would come with Richard, the other soldier in tow. He would prod Gruffudd's hip in order to judge his strength – 'You will live!' he'd say before leaving.

He had tried to question Gruffudd once, and when Gruffudd refused to answer he had threatened to have him put back in the pit. Gruffudd said nothing, but turned his back on the knight. Then he had got hold of his hair and forced him to sit upright and look at him.

'Answer me you mule! Answer!' He had laughed – a loud, mad cackle. 'Answer or your friend the Welshman will be back!'

Although Gruffudd continued to defy his command, remaining silent, the Welsh guard did not return, and Philip stopped his questioning, choosing rather to mock and threaten each time he visited. It became apparent that all apart from the knight and the same two soldiers were forbidden from visiting the hut and its precious prisoner. Gruffudd occasionally glimpsed the guard who marched to and fro in front of the hut – but he had other prisoners to look out for. Gruffudd would hear voices and footsteps passing the opening every day, sometimes the sound of horses moving, hounds barking, women chatting, sheep, pigs and goats. The sound of men at work, girls shouting – once or twice he thought he could hear people speaking in Welsh, but none of them, as far as he could tell, had ventured near the opening to his prison.

None of them came near during the first few months – he had lost count of the days. Then one afternoon, following a busy morning when he had heard the sound of hooves, and heavily laden soldiers rushing to and fro, Gruffudd became aware of a whispering Welsh voice. It came from the opening. 'Hey, are you awake? Gruffudd ap Cynan?'

Gruffudd, fearing that it could be the Welsh guard again, remained on the floor, keeping still and silent.

'Are you being fed?' the voice at the opening persisted. Gruffudd realised that he had not heard this voice previously.

'I work here . . .' said the voice, suddenly becoming more urgent. 'I must go, the watchman is on his way back, here, take this!'

The sound of something falling beside him. Gruffudd remained still, the pain in his limbs throbbing. When he tried to turn and ease the pain it only caused the ache to move from one limb to the other. He was nothing but skin and bone, lying there on the hard earthen floor. Every bone in his body ached. After a while, he turned again, trying to find a bearable position, and faced the opening. He opened his eyes, and there beside him was a golden apple.

Someone had been brave enough to risk punishment in order to give him the apple. Suddenly he clutched the fruit, staring at its golden skin, the realisation that someone had given him the apple slowly becoming a strange sensation. He hid the apple in his loose sleeve. The following morning, he took a bite out of it and slowly chewed before swallowing, relishing the sweetness on his tongue. He would take a bite each day. He wanted to thank the apple-giver, if only he would return.

He had only eaten half the fruit when, on the third day, Philip and his men came hurriedly in. The shackles were opened, the soldiers got hold of him, and they followed the knight outside. They passed several buildings. With the sun blinding his weak eyes, Gruffudd struggled to see, but he could hear the sound of men working from within. Voices called out, mocking. He heard the English word king being shouted. Other men shouted in French, and Philip answered. Then came another voice – *'Oedd y melyn yn felys, Gruffudd?'* A

Welsh voice: 'The apple? Good eh?' The person who had thrown him the apple! Gruffudd turned his face slightly as he was dragged along the lower bailey, with the sun at his back and with Normans looking on. Through his half-closed eyes he could just make out a tall, fair-haired man – had he waved his hand? Then another Latin voice – 'Why can't we see him die here?' Gruffudd recognized the voice – the Welsh guard. Philip paused as if to answer, but thought better of it, and ushered them on towards the main gate of the castle.

There at the gate were a group of soldiers, and in their midst, in his blue cloak, Hugh's huge frame appeared. He came towards them, talking briefly to Philip in French, then looked at Gruffudd.

'You have grown old Gruffudd ap Cynan, in just a couple of months!' He smiled. 'But you seem sadly dignified . . . and pathetic. Today you are leaving my care; from now on you will be the ward of Robert of Rhuddlan. Your life will be in his hands.'

His beady eyes stared at Gruffudd. 'If you were my prisoner, you would be allowed to live. However, you would have to give up the stubbornness, and bow to a better, more civilized master . . .'

He backed away suddenly remembering how the prisoner had spat at him. He pressed his fat hands together and turned to Philip. 'See how every man will choose his path – to thrive and ascend to high things, or choose to be ruined . . .'

'I agree Sir.' Philip thrust his fist into Gruffudd's chest. 'We know which path this one chose!'

Gruffudd stared at the baron in contempt. The short

distance had tired him, he could not stand without the support of the soldiers. He wanted to curse the baron, he wished he could call on Saint Columba to curse him and his men, the castle at Chester and all Normans, but he remained quiet. Ignoring the man showed more strength. Raising his face, he looked at the blue sky, the clouds – ships sailing between Wales and Ireland . . . from Aberffraw to Port Láirge . . . Gruffudd smiled, defying the baron.

Hugh walked away slowly, his thin voice sounding a little less certain. 'Take him, Philip, take him to the Rhuddlan's men . . . get him away from me . . .!'

Gruffudd was rushed through the gateway – his feet hardly touching the path, his head spinning. A host of armed men stood outside the gate, waiting. He was dragged along the line, orders given in French. They stopped near a chestnut mare. Edric released one of the manacles from one of his ankles, but was stopped from removing the other. Then the two soldiers pushed Gruffudd onto the back of the mare, almost tipping him over the other side, his thin body too weak to help. He was held there by his leg, hanging over the side, while the soldiers shouted, enjoying the spectacle, mocking. Gruffudd felt the remains of the apple he had hidden in his sleeve slip and fall. Richard grabbed his arms to straighten him, then Philip came over and dug his nails into his thin arm. 'Who gave him the apple?'

'It's the first time I have seen it, sir,' said Edric, and Richard shook his head.

'I'll find out who did this . . .' Philip snarled, stamping the apple into the dirt. Gruffudd stared at the ground.

'You will find,' added Richard, 'that your time here in Chester was heaven on earth!' He let go of Gruffudd's arm. 'Fix the bonds on both ankles, and join them under the mare's belly – that way he won't fall.'

Philip was joined by another knight, a tall man armed with a long vicious-looking sword. Philip turned to him, and spoke in Latin, 'He was once a king.'

The tall knight looked at Gruffudd. 'He's a prisoner,' he said. 'Is he ready to leave?'

'He is, as you can see, alive and without injury' nodded Philip, making it clear that Gruffudd was able to follow their conversation.

'Yes,' the knight raised his voice. 'A bit rickety perhaps?' More laughter.

'I transfer the responsibility over to you now . . .' Philip measured his words, 'to you and your master – Robert of Rhuddlan.'

Philip turned his back and, flanked by the two soldiers, he returned through the castle gate.

With one swift movement the tall knight brought the flat side of his sword down hard across Gruffudd's shoulders. The pain vibrated through his whole body, and the mare lunged forward.

'I'm Odo – Odo de Lacey. You will call me *sir*.' The man barked, 'My duty is to get you to Rhuddlan – alive. That is all. If, for any reason, you get off the mare, I will cut off one of your ears.' His voice a menace, 'Understood?'

Gruffudd looked at the man – he had just one eye, his hair greying. A veteran, Gruffudd realised, experienced in war . . .

and the art of breaking people with his iron fist. He was one of Robert's right-hand men . . . one of the dogs that had defiled Gwynedd. And undoubtedly responsible for the slaughter of his men in Rhug. Did he murder Collwyn? Gruffudd tried to gather the spit in his mouth, but suddenly another blow across the nape of his neck rocked him again, and he fell forward across the nape of the mare, stunned.

'Answer, you stinking dog . . .'

Another bout of laughter from within the gates. Philip issued another order in French, then the answer was given in Latin, for his benefit. 'I'll get him to talk, once we get to Rhuddlan!'

Then the order was given to start. A soldier took hold of the chestnut mare and headed downhill, with Gruffudd pressing down on the neck of the horse. After a few minutes he regained enough strength to sit up again, the wind cool on his face, the sun on his back. In the distance, he made out a stretch of hills, and just for a fleeting moment a hope rose in him. It turned swiftly to longing; he was going home . . . to die.

11

Opening his eyes, he saw a circle of light. He touched the floor – flat stones and earth. He stared at the opening of a pit – this time in Rhuddlan Castle. Then the latest events came flooding back – visits by Odo and two of his soldiers, determined to make him talk – the beatings and torture – a justification – to break his will.

On their first visit, they had kicked and used their fists on him. Blood had poured from his nose and mouth, one of his eyes swollen so badly he could not open it. But he had not spoken.

On the third day they were back, each with staff in hand. He withheld. But the last blow thrown by the knight had knocked him out, unconscious.

Today it was a barrel of water, his head forced under the surface and held until he felt his lungs splitting, his body becoming limp. His head was raised again, as the knight with the one eye repeated, 'Who are your masters . . . Gruffudd ap Cynan . . . you filthy mutt . . . who are your masters?' His fist in Gruffudd's face. 'You are fortunate that Baron Robert is kept busy at Aberffraw for a while. He will be back . . . and you will be . . .'

Suddenly, the thought of Robert in Aberffraw filled Gruffudd with such rage, he somehow released himself from the soldier's grasp and hurled himself, his head thrusting into the knight's stomach, pushing him hard onto the wall of the pit. The knight, stunned, remained doubled up on the floor, as the soldiers rushed to drag Gruffudd on to his back again.

Silence reigned for just a moment, as the soldiers waited for the knight to regain his breath. Then he began shouting, first in French and then in Latin, 'Drown the dog – now! Drown him!'

Suddenly the knight was up again, pushing him into the barrel, his face touching the bottom. He could not hold his breath; he began swallowing water, filling his chest, stomach, head . . . then darkness.

Something was moving along his face, down his neck. Flies flitting from one wound to another. He raised his fingers; they were wet, with blood from the deep wound along his jaw, the result of Odo's final mad blow. He sat up. It didn't matter; they would come any minute now to defile him further – his tongue perhaps, or ears? He just needed to be strong – not to let them break him . . .

He vomited – there was water still in his stomach. A face appeared above him in the opening, watching. 'He's throwing up – he's just a sick dog!' Laughter and sneers. 'That's what you get – greedy dog, drank too much!'

Above the pit, a high building of stone and wood had been built, guarded day and night by five soldiers. A fire was kept alight in the building, casting light into the pit. Every day, faces appeared in the opening; he was spat at, filthy water was thrown down onto him, and sometimes a stone was hurled. When he slid into sleep, he was woken by shouts in French or

Latin. One of the guards shouted in Latin only. Occasionally a piece of bread or meat was thrown to him. He would not touch the food while they watched, determined not to give them the pleasure of seeing him take the food from the floor like an animal. But he would eat eventually, if there was any left after the rats had been. Sometimes he went without water for days, and then a bucket would be lowered.

He lay on the earth, feeling too weak to remain seated. He pressed his hands across his eyes to ease the pain in his head. The cold from his damp clothes seeped into his bones, and he shivered. He should get up – move a little, sit on the pile of stones by his feet. But he could not muster the strength.

The Latin voice was back. 'Hey, your majesty – listen!' Silence, then a sharp pain in his leg, and the sound of something falling. He opened his eyes to see a burning log on the floor; the men laughed again. He closed his eyes.

'Have you ever tasted burning iron?' More jeers. 'Odo is determined to get you howling tomorrow when you taste it! He'll get the filthy dog barking before Robert returns . . .'

On and on, the jeering and mocking continued.

Gruffudd's mind had stopped at Aberffraw. Had the court dispersed before Robert could reach them? What had become of Gwyncu, Anarawd and Bleddyn? What had Robert done with the palace? Would he keep it as his own castle? Would Angharad join him there? He got up, his head spinning. His hatred for the Normans was now so absolute, he felt no fear. Their brutality meant nothing – he was so weak any pain would make him pass out instantly.

The next day, he was left in solitude. Odo did not appear,

as threatened, for several days. He received no visitors. The usual voices had left, and there was little movement at the opening to the pit – no Latin threats or objects thrown at him. The quietness found him thinking more of Aberffraw and Angharad, more so here than when he was in Chester. Was there any chance of an attack from Gwynedd . . .? No, his men at Aberffraw had fallen to the same defeat as his soldiers in Rhug, or had had to become fugitives. His court at Aberffraw was taken. He thrust his foot to dislodge a stone from the pile, and instantly the pain shot through his foot. If only his brave soldiers, Sitriuc, Collwyn and Cormac had survived; even the castle at Chester would be in danger. Would Robert have dared to keep him here in Rhuddlan then? The thought was too painful; he realised that losing his men was the worst of his pain. Thinking of his faithful army slain filled him with such dread and sadness. Angharad, on the other hand – thinking of Angharad rose in him a strange yearning . . . Where was she? Were the stories linking her to this castle true? She wouldn't be here while Robert was away, and even if Robert was present he could not believe that she would be here, knowing what had happened to him . . . knowing of his situation.

Then another thought struck him – did she want to see him one last time? He remembered her words in Aberffraw – how she was afraid of her love for him, knowing that to lose him would destroy her. To see her would be to open a deep wound, she had been so wise. He recalled his words to her then; he'd been such a fool. Had he not boasted of his strength, vowed that he would overcome any threat? He had promised that she would never lose him. Mercifully, she would not see him again, treated no better than an animal. A terrible sadness overtook him.

Another two days passed, then on the afternoon of the second day the voices returned. He sensed a commotion above in the watchtower. Missiles were thrown down at him once more. He tried to ignore the change in mood, but it was difficult, knowing that Robert had returned. The Latin voice was back, taunting, 'Count the hours, your majesty! The baron is back! Your screams will echo around the castle walls before nightfall!'

A larger portion of food was thrown down for him that afternoon, as if the soldiers knew what terror awaited him – throwing down their pity and remorse in anticipation of the spectacle to follow. Gruffudd left their offerings. He wished he could throw the meat back. He decided to ignore them. He had to hold on to his dignity. He would make them, through their actions towards him, prove their unworthiness as men.

Night fell, yet no one came.

However, early the next morning Odo appeared at the opening to the pit.

'Is the dog awake?'

A rope was lowered, and three soldiers dropped one by one into the pit. 'Two old acquaintances and another to keep them company – they want to test your strength once more.'

Nothing more was said. Gruffudd got to his feet, his back against the pit wall. Above him in a circle, Odo among them, a crowd of soldiers watched. Then the attack came. Leather clad fists rained down on his head. He went down on his knees, shielding his eyes with his arms, fist upon fist, a severe blow shattering his nose, he had to defend his head, he tried to turn his face towards the wall, but one of them grasped him by the hair and dragged him into the space. Voices called out, excitedly. Gruffudd fell onto his back, blood pouring from his forehead into his eyes, from his nose, collecting in his mouth. He felt sick, praying the darkness would come – but these were experienced torturers, doing enough damage without causing the prisoner to pass out into oblivion.

One more thrust, his head against the stone wall. Stunned, he could not fathom for a moment what was happening, then he heard the word *torch*. Suddenly, his eyes opening again, a brightness appeared. The fists had stopped. Through his blood-filled nostrils he could make out a burning smell. Smoke clouded the light, a searing pain shot across his legs, his neck. Voices rose again, his skin on fire, smoke filling his senses. The realisation made him jump; his hair, beard and cloak on fire. He tried desperately to put out the flames with his hands – the men pulled back his hands to stop him. He would not call out, he gritted his teeth, he would not. Flames reached his ears, burning – still the soldiers held on to his arms. He struggled, a laughing face in front of him. Suddenly French words shouted from above, and he was free.

Desperately he thrashed out at the flames, throwing himself to the floor, rolling on the earth trying to extinguish the flames. Mad laughter filled the pit. Gruffudd tugged at his burning clothes, ripping them off his searing skin. The torch was lifted up, and over his head once more, to give the men above a better view. More laughter. Then another voice called out in Latin – 'Gruffudd ap Cynan, ha!' Gruffudd knew it was Robert. 'Throw water over him! He needs to be on his feet by nightfall!'

At first the water eased the pain, but it was just a short relief, then the pain returned, worse than ever, a stabbing pain causing his whole body shake and quiver.

The torch was brought nearer again to give the spectators a better view. Odo was giving orders, the men breaking out into shouts and threats again. Then Robert – 'Did you ever see such a wretched sight Odo?'

'He's ready for tonight, sir.'

'Can anyone imagine that this writhing mess was once some sort of king? Or even a small-time pirate?'

'He's just a stinking dog, sir, a filthy mutt!'

'Oh yes, he's been prepared for tonight! Make sure someone watches over him Odo – I don't want him finishing himself off. I want the pleasure of doing that tonight!'

'He's too stubborn, sir. He won't do that.'

'He's weak, Odo, just like the Welsh. I want him in this condition this evening.'

They moved away, muttering their mirth. One of the three soldiers stayed in the pit for a while, but realised that the prisoner was not able to do anything more than lay motionless, eyes closed, so he also left.

His nose a bloody mess, Gruffudd could only breathe through his damaged mouth, his lips burnt and swollen. His whole body suddenly shook again, pain shooting through every muscle.

He watched as one of the guards turned to speak with

another soldier. He noticed how his short beard was shaped into a point – it reminded him of Collwyn. Gruffudd shut his eyes in despair. How long could he endure the abuse? If only he had chosen to fight at Rhug, he would be dead now, he would have been killed along with his men, sword in hand . . . This was not a fitting death for Gwynedd's king – being tortured, taunted, kept like a wild boar in stinking pit. He had dignity – an inherited honour – he could stay silent. How far could he withstand their treatment? They were devious and clever, not letting him slip into oblivion. He could face death – was that the plan for tonight? But another fear gripped him. Could he withstand a hot iron, in his eyes, on his tongue? He knew he would not be allowed to die quietly – that was obvious. What other terror had they planned? Why did it matter what terrible state he was in? Was it because his death was to be a public spectacle? Had they ushered a crowd there to watch – the castle workers, Rhuddlan, Tegeingl – all of Gwynedd? His resolve ebbed again. He began a silent prayer, keeping his lips still. He recited his prayer over and over, sometimes voicing a certain word, begging for absolution and strength.

Then Odo's voice again – 'Get up, get ready!'

12

Odo disappeared behind a leather curtain concealing the opening to a wooden hut. Gruffudd stood in the yard, his three tormentors waiting. His arms were manacled, another chain around his neck was held taut by two of the soldiers, while the third soldier stood chatting to the sentinel near the opening. In the stillness Gruffudd became again aware of his wounded body. The guards jerking the chain had caused him to fall on his face in the dirt, then he was dragged along the yard, re-opening the sores on his face and hands.

Now, staring up at the tower he became aware of the blood dripping into his eyes. Blinking, he could see the blackened wood here and there along the walls. Then he remembered. Had he not almost succeeded in razing this terrible place to the ground . . . once?

If only he had achieved his ambition to rid Rhuddlan of Robert and his Norman rats. Hugh, almost certainly, would have sent another baron. He might possibly have come here himself to stamp his authority, building castles at Rhuddlan and Deganwy.

He knew that Robert's loathing of him was more than just political . . . more than the desire for his kingdom.

One of the men pointed at Gruffudd's face, passing a comment in French, and the others roared, causing two crows to ascend suddenly from the tower, their flight taking them up, up, across the river, heading for the sunset and Gwynedd. Gruffudd stared after them. Odo's voice – 'Yes, take a last look, your last glimpse of the sky!' He came out briefly, barking his command, 'Bring the dog in!' Then, to Gruffudd, 'There is great anticipation – we want to hear your voice!' Gruffudd was dragged between the leather curtains.

Inside, illuminated by three bright torches, a table was set, with ten or twelve men sitting ready, and just two empty places in the centre. On the opposite wall two soldiers stood each side of a large open fire, iron rods in their hands.

Odo took hold of the chain hanging from Gruffudd's neck and tugged, dragging him to stand between the table and fireplace. The metal of the collar pressed hard into his neck, his head spun, and he had to rely on the soldiers' grasp to hold him steady. As he stood in front of the long table, directly opposite the centre, through his blood-caked eyelids he could just make out the forms of the people sitting: dark shapes, the torches casting shadows. He could make out one elderly woman sitting there.

The company pointed and sneered, mocking his burnt hair and beard, jeering. The woman bowed her head. Could she be the baron's mother? Robert was not there.

'Has anyone seen such a fine king?' Odo scoffed. 'I'm sorry – is the filthy dog too near the table?' Another jerk backwards. Gruffudd fell, but got up quickly, standing upright, his head erect. The guests began conversing among themselves, ignoring him; he heard the words, but did not listen. Then he heard a Welsh voice, and the word *brenin*, king, being repeated. Suddenly he became aware of one face, the reddish hair and beard, the tall, narrow forehead. Meirion Goch! Gruffudd could feel the heat of his blood rushing . . .

'They couldn't get him to talk in Chester . . .' Odo nodded towards the two soldiers standing near the fire. 'But I'm sure he'll honour us with his words.'

Then the door at the far end of the hall opened, and Robert entered. Following him, holding onto his hand, was a tall, fair-haired lady. Gruffudd held his breath; even from this distance, he knew instantly who she was. She came forward and sat with Robert, with her face in the light.

'Angharad!' he said through his bloodied lips.

'What did you say?' Odo turned to him.

13

Thirty minutes or more had passed, with Gruffudd standing near the fire, Odo still holding onto the chain, and not a word from Robert. The company had eaten. Robert called for fruit, more drink, a song. Only once had Angharad glanced his way; had Robert told her who the prisoner was? Gruffudd could not believe she could sit there composed, if she knew the identity of the prisoner. Of course, she would never recognise him, at least he could be thankful for that. He did not want her to see him this way, and witness a pitiful man's death, brought to a mocking end. He did not want her sympathy or tears. He didn't know what she felt. After all, her brothers had been conspirators . . . part of Robert's plan.

But she had loved him. She had agreed to become his wife – he could not believe she had deceived him. Her words . . . they were genuine, their time in Aberffraw precious. He blinked several times, trying to clear his vision. He looked at her again – there in a blue gown, her hair loose. She reminded him of the first time he had seen her, here in the hall at Rhuddlan castle. But this hall was a new building, the old hall had been burned to the ground . . .

Sadness welled in him again. Looking at her brought a new weariness. He shut his eyes. He had to be strong for what was to come.

Odo moved uneasily, and one of the soldiers began silently tapping the floor with the iron rod. Having been ignored for too long, Odo exhaled with a gentle growl, then let go of the chain, letting it fall to the ground. Robert looked up.

The baron stood up, and addressed the guests in French. Gruffudd heard the name Odo de Lacey several times, but not his own name. He glimpsed at Angharad, looking for any sign that she knew who he was. But her head was bowed, looking into her cup. Then Robert turned to speak in Latin.

'My good nobleman is ready to entertain us, by introducing us to this . . . wretched creature.' A few smirks, but Angharad's head remained bowed. 'Odo tells me that he is a most awkward prisoner.' Another pause, and more mirth. 'But Odo has never failed to tame a single prisoner . . . not even a stubborn, impudent dog such as this.' His voice rose. 'Did you realise that such a sore as this one dares to defy the authority of a nobleman, a lord and even the king!' He stopped, wiped his mouth on the edge of his sleeve. 'Odo, has he spoken yet?'

'No, sir, he refuses to respond . . .'

'But he is tamed?'

The knight sniggered again, jerking the chain, forcing Gruffudd's head to drop as if in obedience. 'Oh yes, but he remains obstinate, refusing to show respect to his baron sir.'

'Well, I think then it must be our duty as good Christians to teach him humility . . . before he meets his redeemer.'

'He's just a stinking dog, sir.'

'Mind your words, Odo, there are fine ladies present.' He

turned to Angharad. 'Does this spectre frighten you?'

She looked at Robert and asked, 'Is he a Welshman?'

Gruffudd had never heard her speak Latin. Her voice added to his despair.

The baron smiled. 'He sometimes chooses to be a Welshman.'

'What . . .' Angharad paused. 'What crime did he commit?'

'Crime? Crimes! He is a war prisoner and a dangerous fool . . . uncivilized.' He grasped her wrist. 'Come, let us have a good look at him . . .'

'I would rather not, my lord.'

'Come, it will be an interesting experience.'

'But I do not wish the experience, sir.'

'Are you afraid?'

'No.'

'Then I want you to come, I demand you take a good look at him.' He grasped her arm tighter, and she got up without another word. Gruffudd watched as she followed Robert along the back of the table. The old woman spoke to her softly. Gruffudd realised she was the servant who had accompanied Angharad at Aberffraw.

As they both crossed the hall, Gruffudd suddenly had the urge to escape – at least then they would be forced to kill him swiftly, then he would not have to endure the burning irons here in the presence of Angharad. He turned his head, glimpsing at the opening.

'Tighten your grip, Odo, in case this beast has a mad idea . . .'

Odo twisted the chain around his fist. Robert called for a torch, and one of the guards rushed to obey, holding it above

Gruffudd. Robert stopped a couple of steps from Gruffudd's face, still grasping Angharad's wrist. Gruffudd noticed how the girl's eyes filled with sadness. Gruffudd turned his eyes to the floor.

'Did you encounter such a sight, Angharad? Such an ugly, deformed face?'

Angharad remained silent.

'Well?'

'He has suffered terribly, my lord.'

'Undoubtedly . . . but he still has not shown remorse. He has too much pride, lacks humility still . . . Am I correct Odo?'

'Yes, sir.'

Gruffudd watched Angharad's free hand, held tightly by her side, the fingers flexing and stretching, plucking at her gown.

'Who is it?' she asked.

A moment's silence, then, 'Just a pirate,' the baron whispered.

Odo laughed, Meirion Goch joining in the guffaws. The fingers twisting, the knuckles white.

'A pirate?' Her voice quivering.

'Yes, why, do you know of any pirates?'

'I don't recognise this face. My lord, why do you wish me to see this man?'

'Why should you take a good look at him? Well, because it's the last time you will ever see him.'

'Therefore, I should recognise him? Do I know this man?'

'Do you? Take a good look.'

'Sir, please,' her voice shrill, 'please do not torment me.

Who is he? Give me his name!'

'Ah – just think of him as a criminal, who has started on his journey towards his deserved execution.'

'I can't – you have made me uneasy . . . you scare me.' She escaped the baron's grip and hurled herself forward, taking the prisoner's arms – 'Who are you? Your name . . .' Gruffudd could see the terror in her eyes, her mouth wide . . . 'Oh dear God, no! Please not Gruffudd, not Gruffudd ap Cynan!'

She fell to her knees, her body shaking, her arms holding onto Gruffudd. Gruffudd tried desperately to free his arms, pinned behind his back, the shackles tight, but somehow, he managed to bend his elbows to hold her. He uttered her name, but no other words, and she pressed her face to his chest, wailing.

'Aha – so he can speak!' Odo said loudly.

The baron laughed – 'Yes, and he can say more than just a name, Odo.'

'Should we heat the irons sir?'

'Yes, hurry!'

The sound of the irons hitting the stone hearth. Odo tugged at the chains, dragging Gruffudd towards the fire, Angharad gripping his ankles.

'Angharad – leave him!' Robert's bark. 'Now you recognise him.' The men at the table laughed, but the old servant rushed to her mistress, begging her, in Welsh, to loosen her grip. Robert shouted, 'Get away immediately, you could get burnt! Leave him, Angharad!'

'You will scorch him? He can hardly stand, look at him . . . he has suffered enough.' Her face deathly, she faced the baron, her voice a whisper. 'How can you do this . . . the great Baron of Rhuddlan! Is this how you behave? He is the King of Gwynedd!'

'He is just a prisoner!'

'A prisoner,' her voice shaking. 'He is not a *savage* prisoner!'

Robert spat his words. 'Be very careful, my lady, how you word your protest. Mind any extreme words . . .'

'Extreme!' Her eyes flared.

The old woman held onto her arm and tried to appease her. 'Don't say anything else Angharad, be careful,' she whispered in Welsh. 'Ask if we may be excused . . .' She tried to lead Angharad away, but Angharad tugged her hand away.

'What you have inflicted, sir, on this man – on this king, is both uncivilised and barbaric!' Her voice low and deliberate.

'Angharad! You have been warned . . .'

She interrupted. 'Was it not you, sir, who called *this* man uncivilised?' She laughed mirthlessly. '*You* calling *him* barbaric!'

Robert called the soldiers forward. 'Take hold of her, lest she is injured when we throw the prisoner to the floor.'

They held onto her arms. Odo jerked the chain, Gruffudd fell.

'Bring the hottest iron – one will do both eyes.'

'No! Stop!' Angharad cried, 'Is this Norman justice?'

She twisted, the soldiers still holding her, to face the table. 'Father, Father, you must stop them!' she screamed.

A man got up from the farthest corner. 'My lord,' he paused, 'Please forgive me . . .' The voice of Owain ab Edwin.

Gruffudd hadn't realised he was present. The man went on. 'I cannot see how Gruffudd ap Cynan, the lawful King of Gwynedd deserves such treatment; he has not armed himself against your authority for years . . . and . . . well, he clearly will not do so again.'

One of the soldiers took the glowing iron from the fire, and stood by the baron's side. The old servant turned her back, sobbing silently. Owain ab Einion went on, 'And is it not a worthy custom for the Normans to show mercy towards their prisoners?'

'Owain ab Einion – sit down!' Robert answered curtly, 'You know this prisoner is an exception, I cannot show him mercy, and neither should you!'

Owain ab Edwin paused for a moment, as if he was about to speak, then he bowed his head and sat down. Robert turned to Odo.

'Odo, you can work a hot iron . . .' The knight came forward, grinning, and took hold of the iron.

He stooped towards Gruffudd. 'Now?' he turned his head towards Robert.

Angharad screamed, struggling to free herself. She flung herself at Robert's knees, screaming over and over –'No! Please, Robert! No!'

The baron stared at her, his face twisted.

'Now, sir?' Odo shouted.

'My Lord Robert, I plead with you, show mercy!' Angharad cried.

Then Gruffudd's voice, hoarse and fierce – 'Don't plead, Angharad! Don't go on your knees before him . . .'

Angharad remained on the flood, her voice a whisper. 'Please, sir, for my sake . . .'

'The iron is dulling sir.' Odo again.

The baron continued to stare at Angharad, his face a grimace. He fixed his eyes on her there on the floor. Then he barked an order in French. The soldiers loosened their grip, and he stepped nearer to Angharad. 'What do you want me to do, or not to do . . . for your sake, Angharad?'

'Nothing! Nothing!' Gruffudd was shouting now. 'Allow me my dignity . . . until the end. Angharad, don't beg on my behalf . . . don't go on your knees for me . . .'

Angharad fixed her eyes on the baron's face. 'My Lord Robert, for my sake, do not kill this man, do not burn him, do not defile him further.' Her voice a sob. 'I did not recognise him . . . such are his injuries . . .'

'I'll have to get another iron sir . . .' Odo sighed impatiently. Robert did not respond, his attention focused on Angharad.

'Do you wish me to reinstate him on the throne of Gwynedd? Is that your wish? Do you ask me to give him back his crown . . . for your sake?' His voice bitter.

'No . . . all I ask is for mercy . . . let him live without further suffering.'

Robert stared at her silently. Would the pleading have any influence? Gruffudd could not believe he would experience any relief – not at Robert's hands. No mercy. No more than he would show, if things were different. And although he feared the iron, and death, he had forced his mind to be ready, to accept everything – to defy.

The sight of Angharad on her knees, pleading, derided by the Norman, somehow felt like defeat to him, his dignity stolen. He tried to shout at her – but his words came slowly and quietly – *'Gwrando arna i Angharad* . . . Angharad please listen . . . for my sake – don't beg . . . not from him . . .'

Odo gave an order, 'Bring me the other iron!'

'No, wait.' The baron, turning to Angharad again – 'So . . . I must stop . . . I must not go ahead with what he deserves, for your sake . . .?'

'Can you not see? I'm on my knees,' said Angharad, her voice low and deliberate. 'If you care at all for me . . .'

Gruffudd glared at her, as if at a stranger. How could she ignore his orders . . . this woman, her hair falling, golden and gleaming in the light of the fire, her hands folded, bent on her knees in front of the enemy . . . She had not heeded his wish in any way . . . This last minute, she had not looked at him, not spoken of him . . . Rather she had spoken as if he was merely an object to be pitied, her bond with the baron more of an issue . . .

Gruffudd watched as Robert moved closer, resting a hand on Angharad's shoulder. They became the centre of attention now, their connection stealing the show. Odo and the iron had faded, and the pitiful prisoner forgotten. Gruffudd watched as Robert held a lock of the fair hair between his fingers.

'My lady, your plea . . . so persuasive, and your beauty . . . how can a man refuse? However, I cannot ignore completely . . .'

She raised her head to look at his face.

Gruffudd wanted to scream his protest, admonishing her

for prolonging his anguish, but he decided not to speak to her further.

'His life,' Angharad whispered, 'and my future sanity I leave in your hands.'

Robert stroked her hair, and after a while he straightened, 'For now, I will spare him.'

'The iron?'

'It can cool tonight.'

Disappointed voices rose from the tables, but Owain ab Edwin got to his feet. 'The wise will always show compassion, my lord!'

Angharad got up and the old servant went to her, putting her arms around her as she sobbed loudly.

'Did I hear correctly, sir? Is this dog to go from here with his eyes intact?'

'Yes, for tonight.'

Odo raised the iron and hit the ground near Gruffudd, with force. 'After all that trouble . . .'

'You don't understand, Odo.' Robert's voice was hard. 'I said for tonight, he can go.'

'And tomorrow?'

'I will give you your orders soon enough.' Robert went on in French, and Odo dropped the iron onto the floor. 'But what of the filthy dog?'

Robert made an effort to steady his voice. 'Take him back to the pit.'

Angharad interrupted. 'But he has suffered badly in the pit . . .' she looked at Odo, 'I beg you not to send him back there.'

'Take him to the pit, Odo, now.' He turned his back.

Gruffudd was dragged to his feet, and passing Angharad he avoided her gaze. His refusal to look at her caused a searing pain. Because of Angharad he had another day to face. He suddenly felt weak, he could not bear all this again. Tonight, his spirit was broken, his dignity gone. Somehow, he felt it was because of her.

14

Early the next afternoon he was brought up again out of the pit, then dragged across the yard and into the hall. Odo and three of the soldiers led him to the centre of the room. The covers over the narrow windows had been removed, leaving the great hall well lit, a fire burning brightly. Odo shouted his commands, and the servants scuttled away.

Gruffudd was chained onto one of the great wooden posts holding the rafters, as the knight looked towards the fireplace.

'See – the irons are still waiting!' he sneered, 'and if I were the baron, their work would have been done by now.' Bringing his face nearer, and raising a fist as if to thrust it into Gruffudd's face, he then let his hand fall.

They left him there.

Gruffudd could hear their voices behind the leather curtain, just behind the opening, ready to re-enter when called for. He sat at the foot of the post, his back against the wood, staring at the iron rods, the flames causing his wounds to sting. He closed his eyes, his fear welling – he feared the irons more than anything. He had endured everything, had been able to withstand all their abuse, both in Chester and here. Then a thought came to him; there was one pain that caused him more anguish than the dread of the irons even.

He remembered – the fate of his men. That had been worse than any pain or fear.

He heard a small sound behind him; the sound of footsteps and the rustling of a gown. He stayed there without turning.

'Gruffudd!' Angharad stood between him and the fire. He stared at her. Was she alone? Was it a ploy to increase his pain, or was it . . . the last farewell? He recalled her actions last night, the way she had ignored his command, her behaviour towards the baron. He kept his voice inanimate.

'Did you come without him, Angharad?'

'I came to see you.'

'Will it be your last visit?'

She did not answer. He had to appear resolute, stubborn, brave – he did not want her sympathy.

She came nearer. 'Gruffudd, Gruffudd . . .' Tears welled. 'Whatever I did last night, I did it for you . . .'

'I asked you . . . no, I commanded you not to . . .' He could no longer keep his voice steady. 'Seeing you on your knees begging for my life, harmed me more than anything they could do to me . . .'

'You would rather suffer the iron?' Her head high.

'Yes!' He wanted her to suffer; he didn't even consider his words. But his next words were heartfelt – 'I could have saved myself from months of pain and anguish, if I had grovelled and given in the way you did last night.'

'I didn't expect you to thank me, but I had thought perhaps you would understand . . .'

'Understand?' He tugged angrily at the chain. 'Understand

. . . did you not hear of what they did at Rhug? Of course you know; your brothers were there . . .'

She bowed her head slightly, 'Would it not be better to part as friends?'

Gruffudd ignored her. 'You know of their treachery – their actions at Rhug – what they did to my men?'

'Yes.' Just a whisper.

'My brave men . . . the best . . . their dedication and loyalty . . .' She did not answer. 'No-one can take their place; there will not be men equal to them ever . . . Do you remember Collwyn when we were at Aberffraw? We could not be closer, he was my brother. Sitriuc, do you recall Sitriuc? A giant in so many ways, a great leader. And his brother . . . Cormac? You didn't meet him . . .' He groaned. 'All destroyed, not even given the honour of death in battle . . . all suffered because of the Norman's treachery.' He almost added, *and my folly*, but somehow he could not admit his blame now. Visions of that terrible day came into his mind again.

She was silent.

'Where do they lie buried?'

Angharad raised her head and stared at him. 'Your men?'

Gruffudd saw that she seemed confused. 'They were buried . . .?'

'Buried?'

He watched her face, bewildered. She could not test him now of all times . . . His voice rose. 'Where were they put to rest, where are their graves? You should know; your brothers were there. Your great friend the perpetrator!'

She looked at him, stunned. 'What do you think

happened . . .' her words slow, '. . . were you told your men died there?'

'Where were they slaughtered?'

'They were not killed at Rhug, or anywhere else, as I understand . . .'

He stared at her, as if visualising her words. 'But I . . .' He tried to think why he had believed so utterly that his men had been slain. 'The barons, when I was in Chester, they made it clear . . .' Then his voice changed. 'What does it matter! If they're alive!'

'I'm certain they are alive.'

'All of them?' The excitement made his voice rise again.

'I heard that six were killed, the ones who defied Robert's orders of course . . . but no more than . . .'

'Who? Who were they? Do you know Angharad?'

She shook her head.

Gruffudd sat silently again. Of course, it was hopeless to believe that Collwyn would be alive, or Sitriuc . . . or Cormac. But there were other future leaders in their midst: Sitriuc's brother, their names came back to him – Randolph, Tadgh.

'Robert risked bringing me here, knowing that my army was alive.' His voice pleaded – not wanting to hear her answer.

'No, there was no risk, Gruffudd,' her head bowed. 'They will not raise arms again, with their right thumbs cut off . . .'

His hope shattered again, imagining the humiliating return to Aberffraw, their hands a bloody mess. His Irish men, turning their backs on Gwynedd, sailing for Ireland, defiled, facing shame and mockery. They would forever hold their weapons awry.

He recalled the sneering of the barons – Robert jeering that his men would never fight for him, or any other ever again. Those were the words that he had heard, and made him believe that all had been lost.

'Death would have been less a dishonour.' His words mumbled.

She did not hear his words, 'But it is good news Gruffudd? They live!'

'No!' He stared at her, defiant. Why did he have to put up this act of arrogance whenever she was present? 'No! If they were unharmed, then this castle would be a pile of rubble, and the castle at Chester burned to the ground!'

Her eyes welled up again. He hated her pity, she had to suffer.

'Angharad, will your eyes shed tears, when they gouge mine from their sockets?'

She paused, her voice quivering. 'There is no point, Gruffudd, in me trying to convey how I feel, how I witness your pain and share it. You don't want to know of my feelings, of course not, it is irrelevant. Nothing matters to you now except that you keep your dignity, and the longing you feel for your men; Collwyn and the others. They are not important to me, but I was foolish, mad enough to fall in love with *you*.' Gruffudd dragged his gaze from the flames, and watched her face, as she went on. 'You will never understand this love I have for you, nor will you ever see that your failure or defeat makes no difference to my feelings.' She stepped forward and placed her hands on his shoulders. 'And if every inch of your skin was burned, your body a stinking wreck, your hands defiled – it would make no difference to the love I have for you . . . Have you any idea what it is like to love someone in that way?'

She waited, her wide eyes staring at him. He kept his gaze steady.

'No, you have no idea what it is like to love so completely, it hurts – it forces you to do things that disgust . . . loathing yourself for doing things, yet you cannot stop . . . Remember this Gruffudd, when you think of me and are disappointed . . .'

Footsteps approached the opening.

'So, have we had our final goodbyes?' Robert's voice.

Gruffudd stared at her, becoming aware once more of her beauty.

'Will I not see you again?'

Angharad pressed forward. 'Kiss me,' she whispered.

The footsteps nearing.

'My mouth's unclean – my lips a mess . . .'

She pressed her lips to his, gently. Her body weighed tenderly on him.

'If I had imagined that this was your plan, Angharad, I would have asked one of the servants to wash his face for you!' Robert's voice a sneer.

The girl was shaking, whispering something over and over in his ear, her tears on his face. The baron's voice was imperious. Robert reached over to her and pulled her away. 'Leave him, he is filthy, you might catch something. It's time for him to go.'

He wrenched her arms from Gruffudd. She got to her feet and was led across the hall and left without turning back.

15

He was back in the pit; dragged there yesterday after Angharad and the baron had left the hall. He feared the return of Odo, feared being brought up from there one last time. He had been left, and no one had come to taunt him either.

A piece of meat or bread was thrown down to him, but he could not eat, or rest; he felt uneasy. The wounds on his legs made walking difficult; even resting was painful. Sometimes he sat on the pile of stones, then he would move to rest his back against the side of the pit. His mind was troubled, and he could not be still. Angharad was constantly in his thoughts, making him restless, confused. Her words, her tears, her touch. All thoughts of her weakened his resolve. His fears threatened to overwhelm him. He knew that he would not be able to endure the iron. His mind reeled, returning again and again to his only hope – a sudden death. His only hope of hanging on to his dignity.

Across from the pile of stones, where the bread had fallen, he could hear the sound of scuttling rats. He sat watching the rocks. If he remained still for long, would the creatures find their way to his legs, sniffing at the wounds? A shape appeared and scuttled across, disappearing between the stones. Then came another, and another.

A long time had passed since the last bones had been thrown down to him. The pit remained dimly lit, so it was not night then – late afternoon perhaps. Somehow, he thought he was less likely to be slain during the afternoon or evening, although he might be brought up for entertainment if a feast was being held. Were the guests who had taunted him two nights ago still there in the castle? He had expected a visit from them, but none came. Seeing him enduring the iron or being held in the barrel would have been Robert's idea of amusement, or perhaps a warning for the likes of Owain ab Edwin and Meirion Goch. Stranger still, he had not seen Odo or his soldiers since that evening. Had they left for a few days, only to return to him with their usual ferocity? He realised his fear was worse than ever; he would not be able to resist this time . . .

Impatiently, he stood up, and stretched. He must get a grip on his feelings. He crossed to the pile of stones and sat down. He must banish her from his thoughts. Forget her words, her touch. He must concentrate all his energy on being strong, resilient. He would faint, darkness would overcome – he had to believe that his body would let him slip into oblivion. Refusing food, he would become weak, and therefore his body would surely give up . . . He felt shame – he could not face the challenge. This last challenge – his greatest yet. He got to his feet, looking for a crust; he began chewing. Suddenly voices neared – Odo's voice amongst them. He threw the bread to the floor.

A rope was lowered, and two soldiers climbed down. He was raised into the room above, and immediately dragged out into the yard by the same three soldiers, Odo in front. They marched ahead, passing the great hall, and towards the main gate. Was he to be executed out in front of the castle in full view, as a warning to the Welsh? Would Angharad be present? Would they use the iron on his eyes first, so that everyone could hear him scream – devoid of dignity? They would have a bonfire there; he looked about him and saw a plume of white smoke . . .

A crowd had gathered inside the main entrance; soldiers and craftsmen. A few began to shout at him, some shouted at him in English, others spat. One or two called his name, as if greeting him, their Welsh accents clear. Fear stopped them from saying anything. He straightened, and held his head high. But the effort overwhelmed him; his head was spinning, his body swayed. He lowered his head just to gain composure, and stood straight again – he had to remain strong.

Then he was out, crossing the drawbridge. In front of him he could see the mountains, the river, the mill, the woods and the town. There was a small group of soldiers and horsemen gathered in front. He could not see Robert, and she was not there, neither was her father or Meirion Goch. Where were they?

He was pushed forwards, and placed on the back of a mare – the same chestnut that had carried him from Chester. Was he to be sent back to Chester? No, that would be madness. Suddenly Odo called out in French, and the three soldiers pulled him down from the mare's back again, and dragged him to the front, where Odo sat on a white horse. A chain was secured to the iron around Gruffudd's neck, the other end held in Odo's hand. The three soldiers let go of him, and the line of horsemen and foot-soldiers set off down the road. Gruffudd's head began to spin again, he concentrated on staying on his feet, every step a new challenge. He knew that if he fell, he would be dragged down the street. He had to stay on his feet.

Through the street they went, the iron collar cutting into his neck. People jeered, calling out in French from their doorways. Odo waved his sword at them in jest. Children ran alongside, throwing dirt, shouting at him. A small Welsh voice screaming *bwgan! bwgan!* Ogre! Ogre! The whiff of bread baking, meat roasting. A small child bursting into tears. Suddenly, Gruffudd felt fear gripping him like a cold hand.

He must pray. He forced his hands together behind his back. Staring at the hooves, at the road in front, he begged for strength. He sounded the prayer just loud enough to hear the words, feel their power. Another French voice called out to Odo, and the knight turned to look at Gruffudd before shouting back in Latin, 'What? This one cursing me?' Laughter. 'I hardly think he'll get much luck! But whoever cursed him was heard . . .'

More shouts and jeering, the collar causing the wound on his neck to gape, blood dripping onto his chest. But he remained on his feet.

They reached a turning in the road, where another street joined the first. More crowds were gathered there; merchants in their bright cloaks, soldiers, their weapons glistening, and a few Welshmen gathered in their grey flannel, standing in small groups. Had they reached the main street? Gruffudd looked around but could not see the blaze; the smoke seemed to come from farther afield. He could not see Robert or Angharad amongst the faces.

A merchant in a blue cloak stepped forward, and spoke angrily to Odo, pointing at Gruffudd. Odo turned to Gruffudd, and smiled.

'This gentleman wants to see you scorched this afternoon. He tells me there is a blaze ready, just over there . . .!'

The fire, Gruffudd realised, was not within the town walls. The smoke was further ahead. Odo raised his sword again and pointed at Gruffudd. 'This is Gruffudd ap Cynan, the former King of Gwynedd!' he scoffed, the horsemen and crowd joining in the mirth. He must show them – he straightened; his head held high. More laughter. Suddenly he sensed a movement near him, a small group of Welshmen had moved towards him, moving in front of the jeering merchants. Gruffudd's heart raced, they would not dare . . . just six of them. They stepped forward again, Odo raising his sword. 'Get back you . . . he's cursed, just a filthy, disease-ridden dog . . .'

The horsemen and merchants raised their voices again, jeering, but the small row of Welshmen did not seem to heed his words. Gruffudd saw their feet moving nearer. He glimpsed at their faces, and realised that their intention was to try and seize him. They had no chance, but their bravery touched a deep feeling in him. Two of the men came up to him. 'No, there is no way, don't risk it, you are too few . . .' Then one of the men were on him, kicking him to the floor, and the others followed, thrusting their fists at him, their hands around his neck, strangling him, kicking and snarling,

'You, you and your Northern heathens, you destroyed Powys, you deserve the bile of the Normans – why don't I give you the last blow . . .'

Odo smacked the blunt edge of his sword onto the mad Welshman's head; he fell unconscious. The horsemen rushed at the other Welshmen, dragging them away from Gruffudd. He was on his back, blood in his eyes.

'Get up, dog!' Odo shouted, jerking at the chain, but Gruffudd couldn't get his legs to move. Two soldiers grabbed him and got him onto his feet. Odo spurred his horse on, through the noisy crowd. Gruffudd followed unsteadily for a little, then darkness fell once more.

Slowly, through the darkness, he once more smelled smoke. Waking from a nightmare, his voice called out in Danish – 'Not my eyes!' He was moving. He opened his eyes and realised he was across the back of the chestnut mare again, his arms hanging, his wrists tied underneath the animal's neck. To his left rode Odo, and to his right he could make out marshland, and a wooded area. Smoke billowed across the path. He strained his neck. There at the edge of the path a group of hovels was on fire.

'The dog's awake!' Then Odo turned to Gruffudd. 'You opened your eyes just in time; you see these hovels? Your people – couldn't pay their dues. They've gone for the forest, but we'll get them – we'll hunt them out.'

Odo slowed his horse down, got hold of the chestnut mare, and called out for one of his men to come and rearrange Gruffudd, his wrists tied behind his back, so that he could sit up, and ride.

'Did you hear that man in town? He said there was a fire burning, and here it is. If I was Lord of Rhuddlan then I would not hesitate – you would be fuelling the flames.' His one eye took in the wounds on Gruffudd's legs and face. 'Hmm, I've left my mark on you. They don't know how to treat a dirty dog in Chester, but I don't think you will last another winter there . . .' His grey beard shook with laughter.

Gruffudd didn't hear his sneering. A realisation had entered his head – he was alive. On his way back to Chester! He had not endured the hot iron! A sudden surge of hope filled him – he would live! A new faith ran through his blood – now he wanted to live, more than anything, he wanted to live. A miracle had happened. Was it as a result of his prayer? It didn't matter. They had failed to break him. He felt triumphant all of a sudden. Winter could never break him now!

'Why are you grinning, dog?' Odo brought his leather glove down hard across Gruffudd's face. He spurred his horse forward. The chestnut mare followed, Gruffudd sitting straight backed, a small smile on his blood-stained face.

16

He was put back into the same hut inside the walls of Chester castle, and life slipped back to the same rituals as before. His ankles and wrists were chained, with a long chain connecting his ankles to the centre post. Philip was again responsible for him, one of his soldiers keeping guard outside and another, Edric, bringing him the same meal every day.

A few days after his return, he was taken to meet Hugh in the upper hall. The baron looked at his pitiful state, and almost inaudibly murmured 'Shabby treatment . . .' He then addressed Gruffudd. 'So, you escaped Rhuddlan at least. A feat, Gruffudd ap Cynan, I must admit: no less than a miracle.'

The baron squeezed his lips into a thin smile and continued. Gruffudd would be a prisoner at Chester for his remaining years, and would be thrown back into the pit if he attempted to escape. Hugh gave his prisoner no opportunity to refuse to answer by not asking anything. Gruffudd would not be given the chance to defy him with his stubborn silence.

The following day, Edric brought Gruffudd a bucket of clean water and a dry cloth to wash himself. Gruffudd thanked him curtly, but did not speak with any of the others. When the first frost appeared, Edric brought in some wood and made a small fire in the hut, and throughout that winter, the soldier would bring in wood to keep the fire alight. Slowly a connection was made between them and sometimes they would talk.

Gruffudd had proven his resolve against the might of the barons. Both Hugh and Robert had failed to break him. He had remained silent; he had won the challenge, and now he was able to concede and speak with the enemy. Not with all of them – only the ones he chose, and only when it suited him.

Being less stubborn made life easier, especially with the less important soldiers. He also realised that there were advantages to being sociable with the soldier who brought him his meals and little comforts. He was given one regular meal each day and enough wood to keep him from the bitter cold. Surviving meant everything to him. He needed to strengthen so that when the opportunity came, he would be able to escape.

Gruffudd questioned the soldier. At first his questions were superficial – the weather, the contents of the soup, where he got the wood for the fire. Gradually he learned about the soldier's life. Edric was an Englishman, from the Severn Valley; his father had wanted him to become a monk. When he was fifteen, he had escaped the Benedictine monastery, where he had spent his youth and learnt Latin. He had wandered around the area for a while, before being employed by Roger, Earl of Shrewsbury as a servant in his castle at Montgomery. He then became a servant working for a few of the knights in the earl's army during some of the campaigns against Trahaearn. During his time with the army, he had added a little French to his Latin and English, and then two years ago he had been moved to Chester with fifty other soldiers. His knowledge of the three languages helped him gain his position as a guard in Philip's service.

Every time, it was Gruffudd who asked the questions, listening attentively to the soldier's ready answers. During those early months Edric did not venture to ask anything of Gruffudd, seemingly unsure of asking anything of a prisoner who had formerly been a king.

Edric eventually broke the barrier between them, talking openly of his thoughts. He emphasized that he was an Englishman and that he had a little Welsh blood in his veins, his father's father being a Welshman from Gwent. His father held land belonging to the Earl of Hereford, and Edric's hope was to be able to return to his family one day, and be forgiven for leaving the monastery. Many times, he made it clear that he preferred Roger to Hugh, and he respected his master, Philip, whom he held in high esteem as being both brave and wise, and fairer than most of the other Norman knights. On hearing his words, Gruffudd realised who had given permission for the fire to be lit in his freezing hut.

Because Edric had trusted him with his thoughts and with his opinion of the barons, Gruffudd decided to ask – dismissively – a few questions which were of interest to him.

Were there other prisoners in the castle? Seven. Welshmen? No, only Englishmen. Any Welsh working in the castle? Ten perhaps – mostly craftsmen and servants, no soldiers.

Gruffudd continued to question, the answers giving him

insight into castle life, but he longed for more relevant information. He had to inch his way into this man's trust.

Then one cold evening a few days before Christmas, Edric entered the hut, carrying a bundle of dry bracken.

'Bedding for you – a little comfort during the festival.'

'It'll help keep me warm.'

Edric threw the bundle onto the floor, between the post and the wall, opposite the doorway.

'We got a load in yesterday brought in from Tegeingl; luckily we got it before the snow.'

'A bit risky – bringing me the bundle?'

The soldier paused before his next words. 'Philip didn't say anything; at least he believes in keeping his prisoners alive . . . and the earl doesn't care what happens here, as long as no one escapes.'

'What about the other soldiers?'

'I'd be sneered at probably, and become even less popular.'

'So, why did you risk it?'

The soldier moved the bundle with his foot, straightening the edges. 'I sympathise – you are a worthy man . . .' he continued to shape the bracken into a rectangle, forming a bed, '. . . who has suffered, and deserves better.'

Gruffudd studied the man's face. 'How old are you, Edric?'

'Twenty-two.'

'And I'm twenty-eight.' Gruffudd sat down on the bedding. 'Was it the correct decision not to become a monk? You have a certain religious righteousness about you.'

The man smiled. 'I feared the life ahead of me – being there forever.'

‘Everyone has a fear: something that grips them, a fear that gives them strength but can also overwhelm.’ He looked at Edric. ‘People say that Robert of Rhuddlan is fearless.’

Edric was at the door. ‘This covering has made a difference here, don’t you think?’ He turned towards Gruffudd. ‘That man – I despise him.’ He stepped out of the hut, letting the covering settle back into place.

Gruffudd shouted after him. ‘And his brave knight Odo de Lacey?’

Edric’s face re-appeared. ‘The devil’s servant!’

17

Gruffudd had anticipated that the festival would bring feasting, especially on Christmas day, and that he might receive an extra portion. However, on the day, the castle was quieter than usual. Occasionally he clearly heard footsteps crossing the yard, signalling that the latest snow had disappeared. An hour or so after dawn he heard the sound of several knights crossing the yard, but not of any weapons. He guessed that they were on their way to the morning service. He heard their return. That, and the smell of roast meat, was the only sign that anyone was present at the castle.

In the afternoon, Philip entered the hut, followed by Edric. He stared at the bedding and warned Gruffudd not to push it any nearer the fire. He then explained that his master, the earl – a religious man – believed that Christmas should be celebrated in a subdued manner. No drunkenness or other indulgence was to take place.

'Prisoners will fast today,' Philip went on. 'Hugh believes that hunger will give you the opportunity to reflect on your crime, and repent. Then, he believes, you may be forgiven for your weakness and folly.'

The irony almost made Gruffudd laugh out loud – the fat baron with his huge belly deciding that the prisoners, no more than skin and bone, should fast as penance on

Christmas day. The knight went on. 'Concentrate on one weakness, Gruffudd ap Cynan, your greatest sin of all . . .' Philip smiled. 'Pride.'

Gruffudd wanted to laugh in the man's face, but he remained silent. He had to remind himself that he had won; audacity would not serve any purpose. Rather, he would remain wise and astute.

After the two had left, he did not think of his weaknesses nor did he feel like repenting, but he pushed the bedding nearer the fire. He sat there reminiscing, recalling some of the best festive days in Ireland. As a boy he had been allowed to leave his school at Sord-Choluim-Cille, and spend the twelve festive days at home. Some of the other boys had had to stay as they sang in the services. On Christmas day he would have to be up very early to accompany his foster father Cerib, as he attended the service in the old monastery. He remembered his breath forming small white clouds in the frozen air, the sound of the choir . . . He recalled how as a young lad in the court in Dublin, he would be persuaded by his mother to attend the service at the Trinity Church, and the two bells, their tinny chimes breaking out every now and then throughout the day. Somehow, he remembered how the bell tolls sounded like a plea, drowning the sound of the usual merriment. In the evening, Collwyn would join him, and they would show off their young strength by carrying the drunken soldiers who fell onto the trestles and propping them up along the wall of the great hall.

He remembered his mother, every Christmas night, asking him to come to her. She would talk of his father, recalling certain memories, forming in his mind a picture of his father, Cynan. Then, on the one Christmas when he had taken Collwyn with him to Port Láirge, riding on horseback through the forest, racing to be the first back at court, their sweethearts with them – Máire of course, on his horse, sitting in front of him, he had his arm around her waist. Collwyn, getting back to court first.

Suddenly he remembered about Máire's brothers. He snorted, they would also have lost their thumbs at Rhug! The thought amused him so much, his body stretched out on the bed and shook, his laughter ringing out. One of the guards stuck his face through the covering and uttered something in French, before disappearing again.

Gruffudd fell silent for a while, before imagining the brothers having to explain their injuries at the court of Port Láirge. His laughter burst out again, almost like a live beast emerging – freed from a long captivity. It erupted again and again, long after the smile had left his face, leaving him sore, tears filling his eyes. But it was a relief – as if the laughter had with it, pushed out of him some of the bitterness and desolation that somehow had become part of his being.

Afterwards, when he lay on his bed watching the darkness seep into the hut, he would feel the laughter erupting again. Even when he remembered his promise to Angharad, made on the beach at Aberffraw, that she would be his wife before Christmas, even then, the sadness he felt did not linger for long.

Before he slept, Edric came into the hut, calling out, 'Are you awake? Are you well?'

'Yes, why?'

'The guard said you had a bout of mad shouting.'

'I was laughing!'

'Laughing?'

Gruffudd told him of the brothers' visit to Aberffraw, and how he had suggested they accompany him to Rhug. He laughed again. 'They will now be back in Ireland . . .without me,' another bout of mirth, 'without a date for the wedding . . . and . . . without their thumbs!'

Both laughed, Gruffudd the loudest. When they were silent again, Edric grew serious, 'I would like to be married, but I need to get to London first.'

'London?'

'I've heard that there is plenty of work there with the merchant trade, for those who can speak Latin. And another thing – the barons – they have no power there, only the king – and as I understand it, he's not as bad as these earls.'

Gruffudd remained silent. Edric looked sadly into the pitiful fire, then he turned to Gruffudd, taking out a leather flagon hidden in the folds of his cloak. 'A little wine for you, Gruffudd,' he whispered, glancing nervously towards the opening. 'Something to warm you up on Christmas night.'

Gruffudd drank, the wine warming his belly. He drank again, the heat rising to his head. 'You finish it,' he said handing the bottle back to Edric.

'I haven't had wine in months, and with an empty stomach, it makes my head swim.'

He watched the soldier drink.

'How often do the soldiers get to taste wine?'

'Not often.'

'You weren't given permission by Philip to bring me wine?'

The soldier drank, and Gruffudd leaned back on the bracken. Edric finished the wine and hid the flagon in his cloak again.

'You were foolish – bringing wine to me was a risk. What would be your punishment if you were caught?'

Edric paused, 'A whipping perhaps? What does it matter?'

'Nothing matters if you can stand the punishment.' Gruffudd studied the man's face. Did he detect a sign of innocence, a naivety in his eyes?

'What about Philip? Would it not matter if you disappointed him?' he asked.

The soldier shifted his feet uneasily, then looked at Gruffudd. 'Is there a similarity between us?'

None, thought Gruffudd. Edric was nothing but a servant. But he admired Gruffudd enough to suffer for him. Enough to try and make his life a little easier, just as if he were his servant . . . Enough to give him all the snippets of news. Was there a chance . . . Then Gruffudd realised that Edric was looking at him, waiting for his reply. Gruffudd smiled. 'Are we similar? Seeing what risk you took tonight . . .'

He had expected the soldier to smile, but he remained serious, and moved his feet once more. 'Is there anyone in this castle as fearless as Gruffudd ap Cynan?' Edric added.

Had the wine gone straight to the man's head? Gruffudd mused. 'I don't know.'

'Well, *I* don't know!'

'Philip?' Gruffudd suggested.

'Yes, Philip. Any other . . .?'

'You perhaps?' Gruffudd asked laughing.

Edric remained serious, 'I wish I could be.' The soldier turned and kicked another piece of wood into the fire, the light reflected in his dark eyes. His voice lowered. 'It's time for me to leave. I have to escape the power of the barons, I must leave for London . . .' He faced Gruffudd again. 'If a man is willing to risk everything by moving quickly, then he can get away.'

'Yes,' Gruffudd replied, '. . . if he is bold and fearless. Hugh's lands – how far do they reach?'

'Across Mercia, then south, towards London.'

'That far? A man escaping to London would need luck and a fast mind to succeed.'

'But it's possible?' the soldier asked.

'Oh, yes.' Gruffudd stopped; it would be foolish to suggest himself as this man's companion. The possibilities formed into a sudden feeling of anticipation. He would not show any sign of his eagerness yet; he had to be careful, he had to be certain of the Englishman's sincerity. So he would wait, play the game, he would become the man's friend and confidant, stoke the desire in him to escape, to get away from his position in the castle. He would also have to make sure that he was part of any plan. But mainly, he had to be certain that Edric did nothing to arouse the other soldiers' suspicion, he must not be moved from his position as his guard, otherwise all hope would be lost.

'Don't bring me wine again.'

The man looked up suddenly. ‘But why, Gruffudd ap Cynan?’

‘Listen,’ Gruffudd forced his voice to soften. ‘I don’t want to lose you.’

18

The frost eased. Gruffudd could hear birdsong and the bleating of sheep and lambs. He had survived the winter months. With the coming of spring, his spirits rose, things would get better.

Edric continued to bring in wood for the fire, staying to talk awhile. Sometimes after nightfall, he risked bringing Gruffudd an extra morsel: a piece of meaty bone usually, or a crust of dark rye bread, a chunk of cheese. But no more wine or mead. Gruffudd was pleased – the man was obedient: a compliance which he hoped to take advantage of before the end of summer.

The communication between the two was working well. Edric admired the prisoner; a useful friendship developed between them.

Edric brought him news of the castle: what Philip had been doing, the whereabouts of the earl, all the comings and goings. Gruffudd waited for news of Robert; was he back at Chester? He often thought of him, and the prize he had demanded for his leniency. He feared that if Robert came to Chester, Angharad would be in tow. But then, the thought of seeing her again, even if he had lost her, gave him hope. Edric had no news of Robert or of Angharad. They were too far away at Aberffraw, for any news of them to reach Chester.

He held on to the comfort that if Angharad did come to Chester, and he was allowed to meet her, at least he was in better shape now than the last time they had met. His wounds had healed and the scars were no longer an angry colour. His nose still had a slight bump in it, the new skin over his burns hiding the worst. The aches in his stomach had eased, he was given clean water to wash, and Edric sometimes cut his hair and beard.

He still felt the weakness in his limbs, his head swam sometimes if his movements were too quick, and when he jerked suddenly the chains around his wrists and ankles re-opened the old wounds.

By far the greatest change in him was his feeling of hope. He was determined to be strong, to be as healthy and alert as possible. If there was any hope of escape, he must be ready. Nothing but his own survival was now important to him. More so than Angharad or Collwyn, more important even than Gwynedd or Ireland. He forced them to the back of his mind, in order not to waste his time or energy on the longing that had almost drowned him. The present, and a new hope, gripped him. The present consisted of the hut built into the wall in the lower bailey, the chains around his feet, the post, the bed of bracken, the small fire lighting up the night, the long wait for his one bowl of broth, and the hope that Edric, like the raven who fed Elijah, would come back carrying an extra scrap of meat.

Philip turned up every few days. Gruffudd answered his questions curtly, hoping that his apparent obedience would ensure that he was left there in the hut, with Edric as his guard. Edric became his landline, his only hope of escape.

Gruffudd didn't mention his plan to Edric. He had to wait, to be certain that he could trust the man. When the time was right he would make a small suggestion and wait, watching Edric's reaction.

One evening in late April, Gruffudd got his chance. Edric came into the hut, hiding a piece of meat under his cloak. He held the scrap near the fire, so Gruffudd could see it in the darkness.

'Lamb! The first lamb of the season!'

Gruffudd took the bone and ate.

'Sweet?'

Gruffudd continued to rip the meat off the bone.

'I think they may be a little suspicious in the kitchen.'

Gruffudd stopped chewing. 'Who's suspicious?'

'The steward.'

'What did he say?'

'Called me as I passed the kitchen, told me he had a nice piece of bone going to waste.'

'You went back for it? Was that wise?'

'Well, he might think I've got a hound hidden!'

'Or a mistress in town!'

'He can think what he likes.'

Gruffudd stopped chewing. 'I don't know . . . they've noticed you taking the leftovers somewhere . . . they will want to know where you're taking them next.' The meat was good. 'We can't risk being found out, and you being punished and moved. Don't bring me any more food.'

'Then I'll bring some of my own food.'

Gruffudd considered his offer. 'Only if it's safe. I can go without the extra food. But you must remain here; I don't want to lose you.'

The soldier smiled. 'Why? Why is that so important?'

Gruffudd felt that he could risk mentioning his plan. After all, the man had offered to share his food with him.

He spoke slowly. 'Do you realize that your . . .' he refused to use the word friendship, '. . . your service and company are what makes this prison bearable.'

Eric continued to smile. 'No, Gruffudd ap Cynan, you have the strength to bear this and worse, without my company.'

The man was right. 'Perhaps I have,' he said. He had to avoid being excessive in his praise. 'But it would be harder for me without you, it would be a far lonelier place; only regret and longing for a time gone by, without any hope of any other future . . .' Suddenly the man's eyes flickered.

'What other future have you here?' the man asked.

Gruffudd could not make out Edric's thoughts. He continued carefully, 'That I will one day be free.'

'What do you mean? Escape?'

Gruffudd felt the soldier's anxiety.

'No,' he added. 'Just behaving, being an obedient prisoner, you make that an easy task, and so, perhaps one day, they will release me before I end my days here.'

'That's a forlorn hope.' Edric's voice was serious. Had he succeeded in reassuring Edric? If so, he could nudge a little more...

'And what is your future Edric?'

'I have a choice.'

'Have you a choice now?'

Edric shuffled his feet, a sure sign, Gruffudd had found, that the soldier was uneasy. He went on.

'London is far away, as is your freedom Edric, just as it was five months ago.'

'I haven't . . . I haven't made my choice yet.'

Gruffudd watched as Edric shuffled one foot, then the other, always staying on his feet, every time he came, never sitting. It pleased Gruffudd, it seemed that the man was showing respect. Gruffudd went on quietly. 'Do you recall your words on Christmas night? How you would like to get away from the barons?'

Edric didn't reply.

'Was that the wine talking?' asked Gruffudd.

'No, I often think of it . . .'

'But unable to make a decision?'

'It's a terrible step to take; there will be no turning back.'

'Worse on your own.'

'Yes.'

'Is there anyone else who would risk it with you?'

'I can think of no-one.'

'What became of the other soldier, the one who was with you before I was taken to Rhuddlan?'

'Richard? No, he is Philip's right-hand man, I could never mention my plan to him.'

Gruffudd paused, then – 'That mad Welshman, do you remember how he attacked me? I haven't heard anything of him.'

'He left the castle after you went to Rhuddlan.' Edric

shook his head, 'No, there is no one I could trust.'

Gruffudd laughed out loud. 'I know of one who would give everything to accompany you!'

The man looked at Gruffudd. Once more his feet began to shuffle. Gruffudd decided that enough had been said.

'Don't worry, Edric,' he said, lightly. 'One day you might be moved to another castle, nearer London, in a few years perhaps. By the way, I had meant to ask you about the Welshman – who was he?'

'I knew him back in Montgomery. He has returned there on Roger's order.' The soldier's voice was flat. 'I never can remember his name, ap Rhiw . . .?'

'Ap Rhiwallon? From Maelor?'

'Yes, that's it. He was a relative of Trahaearn . . .'

Gruffudd smiled. 'I can understand his attitude then. I was treated with the same contempt in Rhuddlan, by Welshmen.'

Edric started towards the opening, then turned back. 'I've just got enough firewood for tonight, the weather is getting warmer.'

'The fire is good company!' said Gruffudd, then added before Edric disappeared behind the covering, 'And remember, no more food from the kitchen for me.'

Alone, Gruffudd felt a sudden sadness overcome him. Had he succeeded in giving Edric the chance to help him escape? Was even mentioning such a plan to an enemy soldier just madness? What was it that fuelled his uncertainty? The man's reaction? He would have to wait.

19

Gruffudd walked around the hut, dragging the heavy chain behind him. It was a warm evening at the beginning of August. Excitement made his body quiver, his breath rapid. Hugh, accompanied by a good number of soldiers, had left the castle on a visit to one of the other lords at Malpas, leaving the almost empty castle under Philip's supervision.

Gruffudd had waited two months for such a day. He had waited since the night Edric had rushed in, carrying the broth, having added some of his own portion to Gruffudd's wooden bowl. After Gruffudd had finished eating, Edric had whispered, 'I'm leaving, Gruffudd. I must. I can think of nothing else, it's just as it was in the monastery before I escaped.'

Gruffudd hadn't hesitated this time. 'Let me come with you . . .'

The soldier interrupted, 'Don't ask! I can't! I can do it on my own.'

Gruffudd had planned his words, expecting that very response. Speaking slowly, emphasizing his words, he spoke. 'I was – no, I *am* – a king. You will be awarded – servants, cattle, land . . .'

'You have nothing, Gruffudd! Robert of Rhuddlan has taken every acre of your land.'

Gruffudd had one more chance. 'Why London?'

'I don't know; I've not considered anywhere else.'

'Listen, I know of a place where I could get you on a ship to Ireland. We would be welcomed at court in Dublin, you would be given a good job, far better than anything you could find in London. I can promise you . . .'

'Dublin – city of the Danes! No, they are barbarians!'

'Barbarians! Dublin – the city of the churches. You will never find a more civilized city.'

The soldier faltered. When he spoke next, his voice was less sure. 'I've got London in my head! Where did you think we could get a ship for Ireland?'

'Somewhere on the coast of Gwynedd, far easier than travelling to London.'

'But you cannot be certain of a ship . . .'

'I have never failed before.' He added fiercely, 'I am far more certain that I can get a ship, than you are of reaching London.'

'And you would take me to Ireland?' The soldier replied, slowly.

'I've promised, don't ever doubt my word.'

'And I would be given work?'

'That was my promise. In Dublin, you would be far from the clutches of any Norman earl or baron.'

Edric moved nearer, reached out, and Gruffudd clutched his hands. 'We'll go together . . .to Ireland!'

They both laughed.

During the following weeks, the two discussed their plan every day, deciding that they had to go before the end of summer. They would have to leave when the earl was away on a visit or campaign; the castle would be reasonably quiet, most of the soldiers accompanying their leader, and the remaining soldiers less vigilant.

Edric had agreed that Gruffudd should learn English – just enough to help him leave the castle as an Englishman, then he would be out of the town and over the river. The soldier was surprised at Gruffudd's aptitude with languages, and he spent most of his evenings practising. Gradually their plan began to take form; Gruffudd doing most of the planning, Edric preparing the way. Then there was a long wait of two months.

Gruffudd walked to the centre post, sat and leaned back. He went through the plan again and again, each step . . .

Just before sunset, Edric would bring him his meal as usual; he would also carry a cloak and the key to unlock the shackles. Then at sunset, when the serfs and artisans left the castle, making their way home, they would join the steady stream through the main gate. At dusk, and because so many of the regular soldiers had left with the earl, there would only be one soldier on guard. Edric had assured him that tonight's guard had never set eyes on Gruffudd, and would not recognize the prisoner. The only watchman who was familiar with Gruffudd had been moved to the tower, replacing one of the guards who had gone with the earl.

The plan was to keep west and leave the town through the western gate. There they would keep in the shadow of a tall hedge, running along the riverbank. Edric had arranged that a horse would be tethered, waiting. Just one horse; Edric had stolen a sword from the castle to be able to buy it from an Englishman in town. One horse would be sufficient to carry them under the cloak of darkness along the river and towards the hills of Edeyrnion.

The thought of the journey raised in Gruffudd a sense of great anticipation. The next hour, after all the suffering and hours of desolation, would be of such significance. The next hour would be either an astounding and unforgettable success, or a devastating failure.

He longed to see Edric enter the hut with the meal, the cloak, the key and the news that nothing had changed to destroy their plan. He stood up again and circled the hut, as far as the chain would allow. He had been doing this every day for the last two months in an attempt to strengthen his legs, but his steps were short and slow. He blamed the chain, hoping that without its weight, he would be able to run if he had to.

He pressed his eye to the gap in the wooden wall of the hut, staring at the sky. The sunset seeping through the edges of the dark clouds . . . footsteps crossing the bailey towards the hut. Gruffudd stepped back towards the post, hoping it was Edric. The footsteps continued; it was not Edric. Whoever it was passed on towards the main gate. Then almost immediately, more footsteps, and more again. The workers were leaving for home. If Edric didn't come soon the chance would be lost . . . Gruffudd became aware of heavy rain on the roof. Someone was running past. A feeling of cold disappointment seeped through him. Then his temper flared. He raised the chain and tugged at it. 'What keeps the fool from coming?' he shouted in Irish. 'I will leave this damned place with or without his help . . .'

'Gruffudd ap Cynan?'

Gruffudd turned to face the opening. Edric stood there, a cloak in his hand, he could hear the sound of metal, the key.

'Did you get everything?' he asked.

The soldier dropped to his knees. 'Everything but your food, I couldn't wait any longer for it.'

Gruffudd felt one shackle loosening. He leaned on the soldier. 'You did well. Let's do it – quickly.'

The second shackle was open; Gruffudd stepped away from the chain. Then his wrists were free.

'Here, take the cloak, put the hood up, it's good that it's raining.'

Voices were raised again, as more workers passed. Edric moved to the opening, taking a look outside. Gruffudd tried to follow, but his stride caused a pain to shoot through his hip, forcing him to take shorter steps.

'It's safe . . . what is it?' Edric watched as Gruffudd tried to move.

'Nothing!' Gruffudd tried to dismiss the pain. 'Let's go.'

Gruffudd followed the soldier. Outside it was darkening, the rain heavy, as they joined the workers towards the main gate, their heads bowed against the weather.

'Bring the hood forward over your face,' said Edric. 'We must hurry to catch up with that lot, so we can leave the main gate with them.'

'Wait!' whispered Gruffudd, 'I can't run straight away, let me lean on you for a bit, I just need to get used to it . . .'

The soldier peered at him, concerned. 'Are you sure?'

'Yes, yes, go on.'

They headed towards the main gate, Edric quickening his pace, Gruffudd pushing his hand into his hip, trying to alleviate the pain, whilst hanging onto Edric's arm with his other hand. As they got nearer the gate Edric whispered again, 'Hide your face, and remember – you're a carpenter working on the prisoners' huts.'

Then they were both walking amidst the workers, the main gate just in front. Gruffudd moved his hand from his hip, so that he could grasp the cloak a little tighter; he had to hide his tattered clothes. Most of the workers ignored them, hurrying out of the gate, and towards home. Then as they passed three men sheltering beneath the gateway, Edric realised they were watching him. He released Gruffudd's arm, but got hold of his wrist. Just in front of them an old woman dragged her feet, accompanied by a fair-headed boy carrying a large leather sack, and beyond them four labourers had reached the gate, talking loudly in English with the guard, who stood beneath the great wall, lance in hand.

The men stopped to joke with the guard. Edric slowed his step, Gruffudd getting used to the pain in his limbs. The four men moved on, the old woman and the boy reached the gate ... Gruffudd could see the guard leaning his back against the wall ... a good sign, he wasn't alert ... The guard lowered the lance and started poking the leather sack.

'What's in the sack boy?' The guard spoke slowly, trying out his English.

'Two sets of clothes sir.'

‘Stolen?’

‘Of course!’ the old woman joined in. ‘Haven’t you seen me before? Lift your lance, come on, I’ve got a lot of mending to do . . .’

The guard, laughing, raised his weapon to let them through, and the old woman and the boy hurried along through the gate and over the drawbridge.

Gruffudd felt the heat of Edric’s hand on his wrist; their turn to face the guard.

‘Going out in this weather Edric?’ said the guard, smirking.

‘Just down the lane, I’m . . .’ faltering, ‘just down into town . . .’

‘Into town – got a girl at last?’

‘No, I need to take this one . . .’ The words too quick. The guard moved his gaze onto Gruffudd. ‘He’s a carpenter – he’s being doing some work on the prisoners’ hut for Philip Basset.’

‘A carpenter? I haven’t seen him before.’

Gruffudd felt Edric edging forward.

‘He only began working here today . . . he’s unwell . . . a good worker . . . Philip gave me instructions to accompany him, he was afraid he might . . . we don’t know what ails him . . .’

‘Is that why you’re holding on to him?’

Edric edged a little further. ‘Just making sure he keeps on his feet until I can get him to the bottom of the lane.’

‘He looks sickly . . .’ the guard peering at Gruffudd, ‘are you certain he’s still breathing?’

‘Oh yes . . .!’

The guard laughed. ‘Go on, get him away from here, and

hurry, I'll be closing the gate as soon as this lot have passed.'

Edric pushed Gruffudd ahead of him, across the drawbridge. Gruffudd, fighting the pain in his hip, felt grass and the track verge under his feet, the wind and rain on his face. Ahead of them: the town's lights, the blackness of the city wall, and beyond, the glow of the river . . . Edric's feet rushing, the pain in his legs . . . a voice shouting...

'Edric, Edric!'

Edric stopped, turning around. The three workers were standing there inside the gateway with the guard, watching. Then the guard crossed the drawbridge. 'One of these men doubts your word Edric . . .' The guard's voice sharper than before. 'That half-corpse – a carpenter?'

Edric waited, then shouted his response. 'He just started today . . .'

'He says he saw the mark of a shackle on his wrist, where your hand is Edric . . .'

'Nonsense! I'll be back now . . .' Edric quickened his pace, Gruffudd saw one of the workers disappear back into the castle, the guard shouting, 'Edric, listen to me, just bring him back a minute, then I can prove your story.'

Edric moved forward again. 'He's sent for more soldiers,' Gruffudd whispered.

The guard stepped forward again, then Edric tugged at Gruffudd's arm, 'Run! We must run! Down the first lane, quick!'

They began running, but the pain seared through Gruffudd, and after just a few steps he fell on his face. Edric stood over him, shouting, 'Get up, get up!'

Then the guard shouted, 'Come back Edric, don't be a fool, listen to me!'

Another dash, Edric's arms trying to support Gruffudd. They ran past the old woman and the boy. 'Why are you dragging the old man . . .?'

The muscles of his legs in a spasm again, Gruffudd fell to his knees, Edric almost dragging him down the hill. His legs would not serve him, buckling under him again and again. Then Edric's voice became an urgent cry –'You are too weak, come on, climb onto my back . . .'

The guard was shouting. 'Bring him back here, Edric!'

Edric tried in vain to lift Gruffudd. 'No!' Gruffudd screamed. 'Just support my weight . . .' They started off again. 'Head for the darkness of that street . . .' But his legs gave up once again, throwing him on his side onto the grass verge, Edric following.

'Edric, wait! Stop while you have the chance! Listen to me before Philip Basset . . .'

Edric wailed, his words unclear. 'Philip!' he said, getting up and heading for the darkness of the nearest houses. Gruffudd tried to get up, to follow him, the rain like warm tears on his face. He heard footsteps behind him, voices very near.

'Edric, you fool!' Then the voice changed. 'Get hold of the old man!'

Hands gripping him, Gruffudd saw Edric's back disappear, and felt the tip of the lance through the wool of the cloak. 'Wait, old man – I just want to see your wrists. Show them!'

The two workers pulled up his sleeves to show the red weals on his arms.

'A prisoner!' The guard laughed. 'Trying to get away in this weather! And what was that fool Edric up to?'

Gruffudd remained silent, the hood thrust back.

'Who is he?' one of the craftsmen asked. 'I don't recognise him.'

The guard smiled. Then the old woman came up to them again, the boy following. She looked at Gruffudd's face. 'I've seen this one before, last summer, he was taken across the lower bailey, taking him to Rhuddlan they were – I can't remember his name – but he used to be a king of a sort, a wild Welsh king . . . or something . . .'

'Yes, it's Gruffudd ap Cynan!' the guard smiled. 'I wonder what Philip will have to say when he finds out about Edric the Englishman and this one!'

Four soldiers rushed down from the castle gate. The guard raised his lance and pointed towards the houses; the soldiers rushed ahead. Gruffudd could feel the tip of the weapon burning the skin of his neck.

20

Two French voices, footsteps coming towards the hut. Gruffudd, his eyes shut, heard the covering being pushed aside, and realised that one of the voices was Philip's. The knight continued to talk. Gruffudd understood enough to know that he was calling another into the hut. Then he turned to Latin.

'See that wretched heap?'

'It's a bit dark in here.' The second voice deep, a stranger. Gruffudd remained still, his eyes shut.

'On that bundle of grass there.'

'By the post – yes, I can see him.'

'He's our most significant prisoner.' Philip's voice changed – authoritative, taking on a mock considerate tone. 'How many years have you been with us, Gruffudd – six, seven, perhaps . . . eight years?'

'I don't know!' Gruffudd replied without opening his eyes. He knew to the day how long he had been a prisoner. But lately he amused himself by fooling them. He pretended his memory was ailing, and he mistook simple orders so that they had to do things for him, serve him, as if madness had overcome him. Acting as if he was a poor demented soul, he hoped their watch over him would lessen, thinking that his mind was too weak to conjure up any more plans of escape.

The hope that one day he would escape was as basic to him as breathing. Keeping his mind sharp by tricking the Norman was important – each time he succeeded, he felt it as a minor victory, and each victory kept his mind from rotting into nothingness.

He had learnt that communicating with his captors made his life far more bearable. And when he pretended not to be himself, he could communicate without experiencing any loss of self-respect. Only occasionally did he suspect that Philip understood his little game. Then there would be times when the line was fine, when he was unsure whether his mind was getting just a little muddled.

His stubbornness had saved him many a time; he'd had to show that he could endure any treatment, and that had kept his mind sharp. It was only once that he'd felt his resilience slipping. It was at the end of the terrible year when he had been thrown into the pit, following his attempt at escape with Edric. The worst part was when he began to fear he would be left there forever.

Philip's voice again. 'You remember well enough, Gruffudd.' Silence again, Gruffudd realising they were staring at him. 'Seven years ago, he was the King of Gwynedd, but just for a month or so. He wasn't cunning enough . . .' The knight's voice rose. 'Do you recall Rhug, Gruffudd?'

The footsteps came nearer.

'Look at his face,' said Philip. 'He remembers it well.'

The deep voice asked, 'What happened there?'

'At Rhug? Oh . . .' Philip turned to speak in French, and they both laughed.

Gruffudd often recalled the events at Rhug. During his time in Chester, he had taught himself to turn his mind to Rhug, without doing so as a penance. Strangely, he could now remember the small seemingly insignificant things well. The gorse bushes above the meadow, the scent of the wild flowers as the early sun warmed the dew. Hugh washing his fat, pale fingers in the wooden bowl. Long lines of Norman horses drinking from the river, their tails waving away the flies. The roar of the crowd as Sitriuc lifted the enormous Norman soldier onto his shoulders. Cormac walking drunkenly across the grass. Collwyn's words – 'Do you want to live, Gruffudd?'

He often asked himself the same questions, whenever he thought of Rhug. Would he have been spared the devastation if he had agreed to the baron's first demands? Would he have escaped with at least a few of his men if he had chosen to fight? Then less meaningful questions formed in his mind – Why were Angharad's brothers present? Was Cynwrig Hir as genuine as he had seemed? Then the recurring question – Was there a connection between the visit Angharad and her father had made to Aberffraw, and the treachery at Rhug?

He had pondered over the questions so many times, they posed little pain or embarrassment to him now.

The deep voice again – 'It's difficult to comprehend, now, that the armies of two powerful barons were needed to capture him.'

'He was a wild one back in the day . . .' Philip laughed again. 'What name were you given, Gruffudd?'

'I don't know.' Gruffudd kept his eyes shut.

'You remember well enough – Western Wildfire!'

'Looks as if the fire has been snuffed out of this one at least . . .' The deep voice sniggering.

'I'm not so sure, this one has a strange strength in him . . .'

'But he's been tamed, his spirit broken.'

'Oh yes, it took six years . . .' He kicked Gruffudd gently in the back. 'You don't give us much trouble now, do you, Gruffudd?'

'No,' replied Gruffudd.

'He tried to escape about five years ago, took one of my best soldiers with him – that fool drowned trying to cross the river, a waste of a good lad . . . it was your doing wasn't it Gruffudd?

'Of course.'

'What happened to this one?' the stranger asked.

'Oh – just got to the bottom of the lane and gave up!'

Getting down to the bottom of the lane. Today, even a stroll from one end of the hut to the other was too much of an effort. The chains had dug into his limbs. If he was to escape again, then he would have to be carried . . .

None of his guards had been as easy or friendly as Edric. Philip had made sure that two guards were on duty at all times, bringing him his meals and entering the hut together, and no two were ever with him for more than two or three weeks. Never for enough time for him to be able to make any bond. However, lately he had noticed a slacking . . . For the last few months, the same three pairs had been entering the hut, and lately the same pair had been on duty for a month or so. But only one pair had shown him any sign of sympathy:

two middle-aged guards, Gamaches and Martin. Gamaches had been Hugh's representative in the staff contest against Riagan at Rhug. He could speak English well, and would tease Gruffudd, going on about how he was tricked in Rhug. But he hadn't seen Gamaches or Martin for weeks now.

'What was his punishment for his attempted escape?' the stranger asked again.

'A year in the pit . . .'

'I bet there wasn't much western wildfire to give him any light down there!' More mirth.

'Oh no!' another poke in the back. 'You were a different man when we got you up – weren't you, Gruffudd?'

'Yes – a different man.'

They didn't know that the time in the pit had almost killed him. Not that they had abused him the way they had done at Rhuddlan – that, perhaps, would have served as a challenge. Rather, they had disregarded him completely, only sending down one meal a day. He was left in isolation, in his own dirt, in the dank darkness for months. But worst of all was the feeling of complete failure and desolation which had almost made him lose the will to carry on. The damp and cold of the dungeon had seeped into his bones during that long winter, a cough had developed, and slowly he had perceived that he might not survive.

The thought that Hugh and Philip would keep him there forever became unbearable: however, thinking of their treatment of him gave him a new challenge. He would survive, struggling to his feet each day, he forced himself forward, day by day, not letting himself lie on the damp floor except to sleep, standing on his feet, leaning his back against the driest wall of the pit. He devoured all the food he was given, he walked every day around his cell, he prayed solemnly, and each morning and evening he would recite the prayers he learnt in Sord-Choluim-Cille. He took oaths, swearing angry promises that one day he would escape, and then return and destroy both Rhuddlan castle and the fort at Chester, before, of course, marrying Angharad. That was before the news of her and Robert had reached him.

'And the Earl of Chester has allowed him to live?' The deep voice again.

'As you see,' replied Philip.

'Just because he once was a king?'

'Robert of Rhuddlan – he almost killed him. Somehow, he came back here, in a very bad state, but he was alive . . . just.'

'A miracle? Is he very pious?'

Philip laughed again. 'Godly? Would you say so, Gruffudd?'

'I am.'

Philip roared again. 'No doubt – and of course he has an angel watching over him . . .'

Gruffudd opened his eyes. The covering over the opening had been pulled to one side, so that more light could enter, hurting his eyes. He saw the stranger in armour standing near Philip.

'I knew mention of the angel would make you open your eyes!' He stepped aside to give Gruffudd a better view of the stranger. 'This is Henry de Courcy. He'll be taking my place for a few months; he will take charge of you, Gruffudd ap Cynan.'

Gruffudd stared at the knight. He was short and slight, his face cleanly shaven. He could make out the usual arrogance of the Norman knight in his small, hard eyes.

'Get to your feet, Gruffudd ap Cynan,' Philip commanded. Gruffudd got up slowly. 'There, do you see how obedient he is?'

'So – this angel?' asked Henry de Courcy.

Philip smiled at Gruffudd. 'Tell him.'

Gruffudd paused, then, 'Angharad, daughter of Owain ab Edwin of Tegeingl . . .'

'Yes, that is who she used to be. But now?'

Gruffudd started again, 'Angharad, daughter of Ow . . .'

'Gruffudd ap Cynan, answer properly!'

Gruffudd paused once more, then, 'Angharad, wife of Robert Earl of Rhuddlan.'

Philip had stated it as a fact so many times, he had come to believe it. He had absorbed the thought and mulled over it for so many years, that now he could think of it and not become angry.

The first time Philip had told him, he had just returned from the pit to the hut. Philip had not at that point started to feel any sympathy towards him. The malice with which he had told Gruffudd had almost floored him.

'Of course, her promise to become his wife got you out of Rhuddlan alive; she had to go through with her promise so that you could get out of the pit alive . . .'

He had suspected that that was how he was allowed to escape death at Rhuddlan, but had tried to persuade himself that it was his own will and steel. When he was told the news at first, he couldn't completely believe Philip's words. He had expected to be dragged to Hugh so that he could give him the news of Angharad and Robert's marriage and gloat over him.

Then a month or so later, Philip had told him that Angharad and Robert were in the castle. He remembered that he had decided on his action – he would smile gracefully and keep silent. But he was not given the chance. Instead, Angharad's old servant came to see him, just standing outside the hut staring at him. He asked if the story was true; had the wedding taken place? But the old woman did nothing but stare at him for a while, before leaving again. She returned on several occasions – twice or maybe three times a year – she would not speak, she would watch him, as if she needed assurance that he was alive and well. Had an agreement been made? Was it part of a marriage contract? At first the thought made him angry, but as time passed the feeling eased; whatever choice she had made, it made life easier for him. He hadn't questioned Philip, even when the relationship between them had eased and he could have mentioned her, questioned the knight on her health, perhaps. He had not mentioned her name to anyone in the five years he had been kept captive, until today. Then he realised that the old servant had not visited him recently. Was the agreement forgotten? Not important as time went by?

'The old servant? I haven't seen her for a while?' Gruffudd asked suddenly. Both men stared at him.

'Who?' Henry de Courcey looked puzzled.

Philip chose to answer Gruffudd first. 'She died some months back. I expect they will send another to take her place soon.' Then he turned to Henry de Courcey. 'I told you he has an angel looking out for him! She needs reassurance that he is kept alive and well.'

The stranger stared at Gruffudd again. 'It seems that he will be here for a long while then.'

'Oh yes, as long as his angel can weave her spell over the Earl of Rhuddlan, and while Hugh remains in this castle.'

'At Winchester we make good use of significant prisoners.'

'He's too weak to do any work,' said Philip hurriedly; he did not like the new man's tone.

'That is not what I meant. We use them as a warning to others who might . . . Well, we leave them in their chains in town, in the gateway, or near the Church. An effective way of warning others who hold any notions of uprising . . .'

Philip paused thoughtfully. 'There is no need here in Chester, the people are loyal to Hugh.'

'Excellent! However, matters could change quickly when . . .' The knight glanced at Gruffudd, wondering if his next words were wise to utter in front of the prisoner. 'Things might change when the king dies. And as we know from the reports that reach us from Rouen – it won't be long . . .'

'Rumours have it that he has been at death's door for several months now.' Philip needed to make it clear to this new knight that Chester was also in contact with the king's court.

'True, but had you heard that he has been very generous lately? The monasteries have been fortunate . . .'

Philip didn't answer.

'It's the usual sign as great men see the shadow of death

encroach . . . No, if he sees the end of this summer, he will not see another Christmas. His kingdom will be divided this winter.' The knight turned towards Gruffudd again, his eyes dark against his pale skin. 'Just think of the opportunities that would give a king such as you! If only you were free, healthy and strong and the head of a powerful army . . . and wise . . .' he scoffed, 'and a miracle happened.'

Philip turned to speak in French with the knight. Gruffudd guessed that they were talking about the king's sons. Was it Robert who would succeed his father?

'Ha! So, it seems not all of the court's gossip reaches Chester!' The knight went on in Latin again, in order to impress on the prisoner that he was better informed than Philip, and that he would not follow Philip's actions. He would make his own decisions. He then reverted to speaking in French, and Gruffudd struggled to keep up with the conversation. Understanding only something about Robert and his brother William, William being the likely successor, he also made out the word *war*.

The two knights turned towards the opening. Philip remained silent, while Henry de Courcey turned back to look at Gruffudd. 'We'll get to know each other, little king!' He turned to ask Philip, 'How old is he?' Philip did not answer. Then they left.

It was apparent that the talk of the king's impending demise had had an outcome. Philip did not usually leave as abruptly. But for Gruffudd the news instilled in him a sudden interest. On the king's death, would the Norman kingdom be thrust into turmoil? He had understood that the conflict between the brothers would mean a rift between the barons. Hugh and Robert would almost certainly stay together, but what of Roger of Shrewsbury? Edric had once told him that Roger's strength was greater than that of Hugh, but he had his doubts. He smiled. If the barons were to take up arms against each other, then the men of Gwynedd could surely take advantage of the conflict. Could they push the Normans out of Gwynedd? Would they come as far as Chester? It was strange that Philip had allowed the man to prattle on, giving him important information. A year or so ago, Philip would never have allowed such careless talk. Was it a sign that Philip regarded his prisoner as helpless, without any hope of a future outside the hut?

Gruffudd smiled. He had to start walking again, every day; he had to strengthen his legs. He dragged his feet over to the post, stopped and then continued as far as the chain would reach towards the outer wall. But just four extra steps caused the shackle to cut into the skin, and he had to stop. He fell, groaning, to the floor.

21

The autumn sun was warm on his face, warming his bones through his thin, woollen clothes. The years spent in the darkness of the hut, and the lack of nourishing food, had weakened his eyes. Today he had been taken outside, into the town for the tenth time, but the sun still hurt his eyes, and he kept them shut. He was almost completely blind if the sun shone. This fact was almost worse than seeing the shackles sink deeply into his wrists and ankles, the pain of movement unbearable.

At least he was out of the castle, and although the movement caused him discomfort, being outside, watching life on the street, gave him some little hope. First, he was carried down the hill from the castle by four soldiers, and put to sit in the clearing in front of the church. His spirits had been raised a week earlier – Philip had entered the hut to tell him of the Norman king's death. It was his last meeting with Philip. One of the guards had informed him that Philip had left with Hugh and his army across Mercia and towards London. Gruffudd knew the reason; he didn't have to ask. The next day Gamaches had entered the hut, carrying Gruffudd's meal. He was alone and waited to talk with Gruffudd, both speaking in English.

'Martin not with you today?' Gruffudd had asked.

'He left with the earl.'

'But not you?'

'I'm older than Martin.'

'I hadn't realised.'

'I have fifteen years on him; a few experienced soldiers are needed here.'

Gruffudd ate the cold broth. He couldn't remember the names of the sons; now that their father, the king, was dead, he wanted more information, but decided against questioning the soldier directly. He would continue to feign ignorance and innocence. 'Has the earl gone to gain himself more land?'

The soldier laughed. 'You understand nothing, do you?'

'I only have the post as company!'

Gamaches smiled, 'Did you not know that the old king had two sons . . .'

'Then he has more than I have.' His voice full of gloom.

'Than you will ever have.' The soldier laughing again.

'Ah, you never know – I might be pardoned by the new king!' Gruffudd took a sip of water. 'Ah, what does it matter! Who needs sons?'

'True, what have you to leave any offspring anyway? Just shackles and chains.'

'You're right.' He gazed at the empty bowl, then raising it, he pushed his face into it, licking the last drops of broth, his mirth and delight hidden. The mighty Norman barons in conflict, far from Gwynedd and Powys. It was a perfect opportunity for the Welsh. But where was Robert of Rhuddlan? What was he up to? Making his voice light he raised his head, 'Then I expect Robert of Rhuddlan will be coming here to defend Chester?'

The soldier stared at him, the smile gone. 'I don't know.'

Robert did not appear, the defence of the castle being given to Henry de Courcy. At first, Gruffudd couldn't work out why Hugh had chosen Henry, rather than the older, more experienced Philip.

Not that Gruffudd cared who had the responsibility. Henry had given the order that Gruffudd was to be carried out of the castle to the town centre every day. He was left there, until the hour before sunset, as a warning to all those who had notions. Henry had explained his reasoning to Gruffudd on the first day. Listening to him, Gruffudd had felt such joy, he had failed to hide the smile, and had nodded at the end of each of Henry's sentences, until the knight had struck him across his face with his hand, and shouted his annoyance in Latin, 'Don't look so pleased, get that smile off your face . . . and don't feign madness . . . I understand your tricks.'

Gruffudd then understood why it was Henry who had been chosen to guard the castle rather than Philip. Henry was to Hugh as Cormac had been to him.

Then Henry had ordered Gamaches, accompanied by three soldiers, to take Gruffudd on a rough stretcher down into the town, to the clearing in front of the church, where the four would stay on watch all day. Gamaches, the leader, would explain to passers-by who Gruffudd was.

The place was busy, noisy – people shouting at him, hundreds of them it seemed to him – his head was pounding. A few threw things at him, and sometimes someone would venture behind the soldiers, throwing blows at him. Gamaches would shout, and warn them to keep back, but he did little to stop the spitting and the curses that were thrown in his direction. Gruffudd kept his eyes shut; he might have opened them had he heard a Welsh or Irish voice, but his eyes remained shut, his head held high.

That evening when sleep overtook him, the nightmares came, one following the other, each one ending with him in a heap on the floor, old, crippled and blind, the crowd jeering, and blows striking his head. He woke in a cold sweat, his head throbbing.

But a hope grew in him, that someone, perhaps, who had watched from afar, would eventually be able to convey a message to the men of Gwynedd or Ireland . . .

On the second day, he was taken to the same spot, and the hope welled inside him. The news of his appearance had spread; more people came to take a glimpse at him. It was good, and he could take the blows and jeering while listening out all day for the sound of a Welsh voice. But he heard none. The only voice he heard that did not rile him was a rough voice behind him somewhere – 'We have it worse, old Welshman, we are starving to death . . .' Gamaches explained that the voice belonged to a former slave, who had been released because of old age, and was begging near the church door.

On the third day, the rough voice was joined by more beggars; they made their way to where Gruffudd was. One of the soldiers sent them away, his lance hitting out. Then they were back, picking up items of rubbish thrown at Gruffudd, scraps of food. The soldiers threatened them with a beating, Gamaches telling the soldiers to leave them, adding some words in French that amused the others. He spoke again, this time in English, so that the crowd would understand.

‘Let them eat – at least the scraps will stop stinking in the street. They won’t be here once the winter months arrive . . .’

By the fourth and fifth day, he was less of a spectacle, and by the time a week had passed no one bothered to come and stare at him, or throw their curses. The old slaves returned to their former begging sites.

Once it rained all day, and two of the soldiers went into a nearby tavern to shelter, while the other two remained flanking Gruffudd, complaining. After each pair had taken their turn in the tavern, Gamaches decided that the four should take Gruffudd into the church porch. They shooed off the old slaves, to get the driest position for themselves. Gruffudd had enjoyed the rain on his face, the drops drenching his sore eyes. He opened them, but he could still not see clearly. While he sat there near the church door a monk appeared, stopped, bent towards Gruffudd and asked in English, ‘Do you repent, blind creature? Do you ask forgiveness for your terrible sins?’

Gruffudd opened his eyes, seeing the dark habit, the hood covering the man’s face. He remembered when he had pulled a hood over his face that evening, when it had rained, Edric urging him to run, the pain in his limbs, his movements unsteady just like a small child.

‘He’s not blind,’ said Gamaches. The face under the hood came nearer.

'Should I pray for you by the holy tomb of Saint Werburgh? Ask forgiveness and pity on your soul?'

'No-one is to pray for the prisoner, monk,' interjected Gamaches.

'Yes.' Gruffudd peered into the darkened face, the hood tipped forward. 'Yes, I beg for her mercy and for strength.'

'For courage in the face of death?'

'To live!' Gruffudd shouted, 'to live . . .'

Gamaches stepped forward. 'Do not pray for this wretched creature, monk, or you will offend the earl, and that will be of little benefit to your monastery.'

The monk stepped away, then before entering the church, he turned back. 'And if I do not pray for his soul, I will offend the Lord.'

The monk did not speak to Gruffudd again, nor did any of the town's other inhabitants, apart from the former slaves.

Today the sun was too strong, he could not open his eyes. Having to keep his eyes shut annoyed him. He also felt disappointed that after ten days of being alert and listening to the sounds surrounding him, he had yet to hear a Welsh or Irish voice. Not a word. Not one word that could give him a glimmer of hope, having been displayed in front of the crowds for ten days. Had everyone forgotten about his existence? Had the six years been sufficient to erase his name forever?

The stench of sweat from the two soldiers reached Gruffudd. They were impatient, the sound of their weapons moving against their armour. He shifted his weight to ease the pain in his bony limbs.

'You wait until tomorrow, you won't be ignored then; the worst will be here tomorrow, you wait . . . the drunks will be out in droves tomorrow.' Ganaches sounded weary.

Gruffudd felt a new hope. 'Why?'

Gamaches spat, 'Tomorrow is St Michael's Festival, the first of the feast days.'

22

Early the next day, Gruffudd was taken to the clearing in front of the church. He was there with the four guards in time to watch the crowd filing into the church for the service.

Before they started off that morning, Henry had entered the hut with Gamaches. The soldier was ordered to give Gruffudd several blows. He did as he was ordered; not putting his strength behind the punches, but enough to draw blood.

'It has been reported to me that you spoke to a monk – take this as a warning! If I hear that you have opened your mouth today or any other day – then you will be back in the pit.'

Because of the blows his head throbbed and the blood had caked on his face. He couldn't wipe his face as the soldiers had tied his hands behind his back for the first time since he had been taken to the town. Henry clearly wanted him to seem more helpless than usual, a warning to anyone who harboured rebellious thoughts.

Gruffudd didn't care, his only hope being that a Welshman, Irishman or perhaps a Dane might recognise him and send a message to Gwynedd. It was strange, but lately he felt perhaps that a Dane from Ireland might be his liberator. He could imagine a fleet from Ireland sailing into Chester, with a giant such as Sitriuc at the helm, setting every street on fire on their way to save him from his position in front of the church. They would roar their fury, thrust their axes in front of them, the soldiers falling. He would be whisked away to the safety of the ship, while another company would plunder the castle. And as the ship sailed on down river towards the sea, he would glimpse back and see the castle engulfed in flames. He would turn his back on that hell and the sails would catch a breeze that would take him towards Dublin . . .

He believed that such a dream was possible, if only the Danes knew there was an opportunity waiting. There was little hope that the men of Gwynedd might come to his aid; they knew of his plight, had known for several years, but as far as he knew, none had made any effort to save him. Not one arrow shot. Nothing. No sign, in all these years, that the Welsh cared enough to take a risk, except for one lonely Welshman – the man who had given him the apple.

What had she done for him? It was strange how seldom his thoughts turned to her these days: only sometimes, when he heard the screeches of the gulls in the tower, or perhaps when he lay unable to sleep. Maybe once or twice, when he had heard a woman's voice calling, and he had thought it might be her. Each time, after listening for a while, he had realised the voice had an English accent.

At the beginning, when he sat there in the clearing, young girls had come to stare and laugh at him. He had kept his eyes shut; his sense of smell awoke in him memories of Máire . . .

He listened, and the crowd came out of the church; he could hear the voices of the merchants, the stall-keepers shouting, banter, and the crowd breaking into a carol, an

English song praising the festivities. Footsteps rushing, the crowd coming towards him, laughing, the sound of celebration. He kept his head up, and although his eyes were shut, his other senses were sharp. He sat there for hours, listening. English voices, French voices and a few lowered Latin voices. Men praising an animal, a bargain, others where the banter had turned to something louder and angrier. The sound of girls in their wooden clogs, shrill voices bargaining for food and cloth – rye bread, doves, cheese and ewes' milk, for wool, leather and linen.

Every now and then Gamaches would call out, 'This wretch is Gruffudd ap Cynan – a former King of Gwynedd. Look at him! His crime? He defied our earl, the great Earl Hugh! Take heed!'

More and more people filed past, sneering, spitting. Dung was thrown at him, or hard clumps of mud and dirt. Anything to hand, bits of rotting vegetables, bits of fish, apple cores. Two or three of the old slaves inched nearer, they quarrelled over the bits that were worth taking. Sometimes the one with the coarse voice crept near and whispered in Gruffudd's ear, 'We have it worse than you, old Welshman, at least you won't starve to death.'

Later one of the others began, between bouts of coughing, 'Look at the little king, what a sorry little king!'

Gruffudd tried to ignore them, they were clearly mad, going over the same old words, over and over, quarrelling over a few rotting bits of food. At least they had placed themselves between him and the crowd, so that he was spared a few blows.

Mid-morning, when the autumn sun had warmed the air, he thought he heard voices, English voices, talking of ships that were about to set sail for Ireland. His heart gave a leap and he strained to listen. He opened his eyes, but the sun blinded him again, then he shouted, 'Hey, are you sailors? Tell the Irish, Gruffudd . . .'

A kick in his face, and Gamaches bent towards him. 'Idiot! Shut your mouth . . .' he spat, '. . . or you will be thrown into the pit again, fool!'

Gruffudd remained on his back, the blow having hit him hard. The sailors were laughing and praising Gamaches's aim. Blood poured from the wound to his mouth, shrill voices surrounded him again. He turned onto his side so that the blood could escape his mouth. His face in the dirt.

Early in the afternoon, Gamaches and one other soldier went to the tavern. On their return the other two took their turn. The sun was hot, and Gruffudd became aware that the sounds around him had changed. There was less bleating, the animals gone, more laughter and yelling. The taverns became noisier. More singing. More sneering and throwing. Stones, dirty water. Sometimes a drunk would offer to throw him in the river, put him in a cask, or even tie him onto the back of a pig – innocent fun. Gamaches refused.

More soldiers joined them during the day, sometimes bringing the guards beer or mead. At one time there was only Gamaches left to watch over him. He propped Gruffudd up, and poured mead into his mouth. They didn't speak. Then the others were back and a few started singing.

Gruffudd listened to the song; he could make out the

words, a story of a soldier and a girl in a wood. Someone threw nuts at him . . . the slaves started quarrelling over them . . . Someone from behind got hold of his hair and tugged him onto his back, then ran away. The song was still going . . . about the girl's father finding them . . . taking out his sword . . . A fly had landed on his face . . .

'We have it worse than you, old Welshman . . .' The voice very near, almost hanging over him. 'We have it worse, little king, at least you won't starve . . .'

'No, we won't!'

'My belly is full!'

'It'll be empty again by Christmas . . .'

'You watch how drunk they are by this afternoon – once the procession reaches the church . . .'

'Then we'll get a feast, what will they throw at you then, little king?'

'More bread.'

'My lord . . . get ready!'

'It was best when he was sitting up.'

Suddenly through his murky thoughts, and muddled between the words of the slaves, Gruffudd became aware that someone near him had said something significant. He could not recall the words, or even make out the language, but somehow a flicker of something had struck him, that he should take note . . .

He kept very still, his ears pricked ready for any sound. An Englishwoman was there with a small boy, her voice cross – 'See what becomes when you disobey, look at his face!'

'No, I don't want to see him.' The child wailing.

'Throw some of the rye-bread at him, boy.' One of the slaves urged.

'Get up, little king.'

'We have it worse . . .'

Then a voice very near. 'Get ready . . .'

The words in Welsh. A rush of blood surged through him; his whole body shook. His lips trembled and tears welled. He began praying – let the voice be real; had he actually heard the Welsh words? He should try to get up, get ready. He forced his eyes open, but there was nothing but the familiar black shadows, and the brightness of the sky beyond. Which one was the Welshman? He could just make out grey forms in front of him. Did the Welshman realise that he couldn't walk? He tried to sit up, shouting at Gamaches – 'Gamaches, can you help me sit up?'

One of the guards came forward, then another, just two of them? Where were the others? The guard spoke.

'I'll help you up when I feel like it,' said Gamaches, turning towards the other guard, both discussing their friends who had joined the procession.

One of the slaves shouted, 'Hey – let the man sit up!'

'We'll help him up.'

'Stand back!' The shadow of Gamaches coming forward, the others receding. 'And you lot too, unless you want the weight of my sword on your backs.'

Two or three of the shadowy figures stepped away, the voice of one of the slaves grumbling, 'This lot, they shouldn't be here anyway.'

Who were the strangers then? Was the Welshman one of

them? But what could three men do? Could they get word out to a company of men? Were there others waiting outside the city gates?

'One step nearer and I'll whip the lot of you!' Gamaches spat. 'No-one touches him.'

The slaves backed away. Gamaches began to stride back and forth, waiting for the others. Gruffudd's mind went back to the Welshman and his two accomplices, if there were two of them. He didn't hear any more Welsh spoken, he didn't know where they were, if they were still amongst the crowd or heading out of the city towards the hills. Their words, *get ready*, could have several meanings.

The crowd noisier, the procession coming their way. Bells ringing, drums, flutes and pipes. The crowd applauding, the slaves rushing past him, heading for the throng . . . He could see nothing but the two shapes flanking him, the tall form of Gamaches and the second form, shorter, the other guard. Someone shouted out, naming the players, 'On horseback, the Order of the Messengers . . .'

'On the white horse – the Bishop . . .'

'The Baron of Malpas and his soldiers. Two hundred strong, heading south . . .'

'The carpenter's cart . . .'

Silently, three forms stepped over Gruffudd's legs. Suddenly two of them fell on Gamaches, the third taking the smaller guard. Just one shout from Gamaches, no sound from the second. The shadows swayed together, then both guards slipped silently to the floor, laying motionless at Gruffudd's feet. Immediately, hands gripped Gruffudd, raising him, a hurried Welsh voice in his ear – 'My lord, we will carry you in a sack . . .'

'To Wales?' Gruffudd's mind reeled.

'Can you stand?'

'I can't see . . .'

Then he felt himself being lifted to his feet, the sack around him.

'Crouch down now.'

He bent his head and knees, the neck of the sack closed over his head, and he felt himself being lifted onto one of the men's shoulders, another of the men taking the weight at the back, as they strode quickly ahead, into the midst of the noisy crowd. A voice shouted out – 'Hay! Hay!'

Another voice, cross – 'Go back! The procession is coming this way!'

The man turned left quickly, and soon, Gruffudd realised they were moving away from the crowd. After a while, the man slowed, and stopped. 'Where is he? Can you see him?' he asked.

'No, but they were selling plenty of hay back there.'

'We have to get through the gate and over the bridge before news gets out.' The man carrying Gruffudd started moving again. 'Go and find him, go back to where the hay was, don't forget the pigs and the mead. Quickly . . .'

'Who are you?' asked Gruffudd.

The hand taking the weight let go and ran off.

'We have to hurry.'

The man carrying the sack began running, making the chains clink. An English voice shouted, 'Wait, why the hurry?'

The man stopped. 'Normans,' he warned, 'I'm on an errand, sir, orders from my lord.'

'What lord may he be?'

The Welshman paused for a second. 'Lord Edwin of Mercia, sir.'

Gruffudd could hear the sound of armour, sweat formed on his forehead, he could not breathe.

'But there is no Lord Edwin of Mercia . . .'

'No, of course not, my stupidity, Edwin of Northop as he is known . . .'

'And your errand is . . .'

'Just been to market, buying and selling . . .'

Another set of footsteps nearing. Gruffudd listened, hoping there was no more sound of armour rushing. But he could hear nothing more than the squealing of piglets, and the Normans whispering amongst themselves.

'Are they with you?'

'Yes sir.'

'You have a large sack there, yet you carry the pigs and casket in your arms?'

Gruffudd kept still, not daring to breathe. Then the man with the sack gave a little laugh. 'I have my brother in the sack sir, the festivities got the better of him, I'm taking him to the river, a quick dip will get him sobered! Would you like to meet him . . .?'

Gruffudd, was aware of the thumping of his heart. What if the soldier was one of the castle's, and recognized him? The sound of armour clinking as the soldier stepped forward. A finger poking the sack, a hand grasping his shoulder through the sacking. A sword ripping the fabric just above his head. He closed his eyes, opened his mouth feigning drunkenness. Silence at the prospect of pain. Then the Norman exhaling loudly, and sniggering.

'What a stink!' He stepped back. 'Yes, throw him in the river! I'd prefer to carry the pigs!'

The man with the sack started off again. 'Thank you sir . . . he's a disgrace, brings nothing but shame to our family . . . a quick dunk in the river will sort him out . . .'

They went on, the other two following, the pigs squealing, just one hand helping to support the weight of the sack. Soon they turned right, and stopped, and the sack was put down. 'My lord, hay to silence the sound of the chains.' Hay was pushed into the sack, covering his arms and legs, and over his head.

'You are not Northop's men?' asked Gruffudd.

'No,' replied the man before tying the sack and hoisting it onto his shoulders again. He strode forwards, the other two following. Then they began running, their breathing heavy. No-one spoke.

Gruffudd's thoughts returned over and over to the scene in front of the church, when Gamaches and the other soldier would be found, and the realization dawned that he had escaped. They would send soldiers on horseback to each of the city gates . . .

Was the carrier taking the shortest route to the nearest gate? They were slowing down again when he spoke, 'My lord, we are approaching the gate over the bridge, is there any chance that the guard will recognize you?'

Gruffudd tried to think, 'I don't know . . . is it near the castle?'

'Yes.'

'Then it's possible.'

'We have hay in the sack.' He turned to the other two. 'Smile . . . we have just been to a festival . . . offer them a sip of the mead.'

They started off again, quickly, one of the pigs squealing. 'I can't believe the news could have reached here before us . . .'

'It's possible, so be prepared to do your worst . . .'

Gruffudd, for the first time, hearing the tension in the voice, felt his body tighten.

Voices calling out in English. The carrier whispering, 'My lord, keep very still.'

'Who are you?'

'Free Welshmen, serving our lord, Edwin of Mercia and Northop, we have been selling our wares . . .' His nervousness making him babble on. Everything unmoving, Gruffudd's heart thudding.

In the distance the sound of drumming, bells, the procession moving forward, footsteps, armour moving. The English voice again – 'What wares?'

The man holding onto the pigs – 'Wool – we sold wool, cloth, and bought these, pigs, hay . . . a sack full . . . mead . . . here, have a swig.'

A sword being drawn, the flat side tapping the sack. Gruffudd felt the cold sweat on his forehead. The Norman calling loudly, 'Your lord will sleep well on the hay this winter.'

The tall man laughing uneasily, 'Oh yes, he insists on hay from St Michael's market at Chester . . .'

Another voice – 'And the best mead!'

The Welshman laughing again, 'Have some more!'

The Norman replying, 'I'll get a drinking horn . . .'

The loud voice again, challenging – 'No! We'll take the flagon, so that you can get on!'

'Well . . .' the tall man pausing as if to defy the soldier, 'very well, it is a religious festival, so take the flagon . . .'

The sound of the merriment returning, the Norman soldier laughing, the Welshmen walking on, calmly. Their feet noisy on the wooden bridge, the sweat in Gruffudd's eyes. The footsteps changing, once over the bridge. The footsteps quickening again, Gruffudd's face turning into a smile, the hay making his nose itch.

The tall man turning to the other two, 'Let's go through the marsh, run, can you see the horses?'

No one made another sound, the hand returning to take some of the sack's weight. Then a low, urgent voice – 'I can see horses, and the others waiting, over there, near the trees, where the hill starts . . .'

'Good!' the tall man groaning, swaying under the weight of the sack, slowing down, bending over. Gruffudd could make out that they were climbing. A strange elation gripped him. 'Who are you?'

No answer.

Again, this time louder, his voice full of joy – 'My friend, who are you?'

'Cynwrig Hir, my lord.'

23

On reaching the others, they mounted their horses and were off, through woodland, climbing steadily before heading for the valleys. Cynwrig Hir led the way, followed by Gruffudd, who was held safely by another tall knight on a strong steed. Then came the others; fifteen or perhaps twenty Welshmen. His weak eyes could hardly see anything – just outlines and shapes. Cynwrig had bypassed every village apart from one: there, Cynwrig took Gruffudd to the blacksmith's hut. Nothing was disclosed; the blacksmith was paid to cut the chains that joined both his wrists and ankles together. The shackles were left, as it would take too long to cut through them.

They went on, climbing up towards a ridge. Gruffudd became aware of a reddish light in his eyes, and realised that he was heading west, towards the sunset. He smiled, felt the wind on his skin, heard the hooves of the horses galloping, and the voices calling out in Welsh. Cynwrig glanced in his direction and laughed. 'We have you, my lord! The Normans, they have no idea . . .'

'How can I begin to . . .' he couldn't remember the Welsh word for *comprehend*. He stopped and asked again, 'How can I begin to work out what this means . . .'

'You could start, my lord, by believing that you are a free man!'

The tall man laughed, and without thinking, Gruffudd joined him. The sound was a strange rumbling, making his whole body shudder; a feeling so strange that it left Gruffudd weak and unsteady.

They followed Cynwrig for at least another thirty minutes, climbing all the while. Gruffudd noticed that the sunset had shifted to their right. Then it was at their backs, and then it disappeared completely as they dropped down into a narrow valley. They slowed down to a trot and continued through another forest, Gruffudd's eyes coping better in the gentle light of dusk. Then they were on a clear path through the forest, where another Welsh voice greeted Cynwrig, then another. The path came to a stop, and they were in a clearing, the dark trees surrounding them. Ahead of them was a tall hedge, and Gruffudd could make out the looming shape of a manor house behind the hedge. A gate was opened. Men came out to meet them, carrying weapons, raising their arms above their heads, shouting their greetings to Cynwrig, calling Gruffudd's name.

Cynwrig paused, waiting for Gruffudd's horse to come to his side.

'Welcome to my home. No Norman has been here for several years,' he smiled. 'They have forgotten that it exists. You are welcome to take it as your home, as your court, to do with as you wish, until your strength returns. I and all who reside here will be your servants, my lord; you will be master here.'

Gruffudd viewed the men who rushed out to meet him, many of them shouting their greetings as they ran. But, gradually, one by one, they became silent, as they saw the condition of their king. A voice asked quietly, 'Does he have an affliction? Is he unwell?'

'Is the king blind?' another asked.

Cynwrig glanced at Gruffudd. 'No . . .'

Then Gruffudd spoke. 'I understand that I seem . . .' he tried to remember the word, '. . . I look very much like a phantom to you . . . and that is what I should be, a ghost, I should not be here.' He raised his head. 'But it is me – Gruffudd ap Cynan, King of Gwynedd!' His voice shook, a fit of coughing engulfing his body. 'I've returned to my kingdom.'

Cynwrig stared at him, but kept silent. He led the way through the gateway, Gruffudd following, noting the silence of the men who came out to greet him. Then Cynwrig halted his horse in the clearing in front of the house and turned in the saddle, speaking directly to the men tentatively standing around them. 'Look at him!' He raised his arm towards Gruffudd. 'This is our lord, men of Gwynedd.' He stopped, then continued, his voice fierce. 'Look at his plight! The Normans may have left their mark on his body, but he is alive, breathing, perceptive. His spirit is unbroken – the Normans could do nothing to break his resolve!' said Cynwrig, taking in all the men standing before him. 'Understand this – you have today witnessed a miracle! It's our worthy duty now to serve him, care for him, help him to regain his former might and strength. We will undertake to ensure that this miracle benefits every acre of our soil; Gwynedd will become strong again.' He paused. 'We are the last stand against the enemy!'

his voice full of emotion now, 'You know as I do – we cannot fail!'

Suddenly a fear gripped Gruffudd; the duty and responsibility expected of him was huge. The silence surrounding him seemed like an age. Then suddenly cheers broke out, the men raising their arms, calling his name, urging him on; their king was back. With the loyalty and passion of his men stirring him on, Gruffudd felt the tears well up. His thoughts reeled: he must address them. He paused, forming the correct words in his mind, then spoke, his voice weak.

'My wounds have already begun to heal; your welcome is the balm that makes me whole again! We are the new beginning – Cynwrig Hir, all of you, and . . . me! We are the beginning of the end of Norman rule in Gwynedd!'

The men roared, their faces alive, and Gruffudd felt his eyes well up again. Then Cynwrig was beside him, helping him down from the saddle.

Inside the manor house, there was great anticipation. He was given a bowl of warm milk to drink, plenty of hot water to bathe, and clean white cloths to dry himself. Two servants helped him; his wounds were carefully washed in herb-infused water. His hair and beard were cut and washed, then he was given new clothes to wear.

It was decided to leave the delicate task of removing the shackles until the following day, when he was less tired, and the women had had enough time to prepare plenty of herbs to dress the terrible wounds on his wrists and ankles.

Cynwrig did not leave his side. All the time while he was

washed and his wounds treated, Cynwrig was there, silently watching over him. The day's excitement had exhausted Gruffudd. At times a great feeling of tiredness came over him, almost paralysing his whole body. But the effect on his mind was very different. His thoughts raced – relief, hope and joy mixed with just a little apprehension and fear. He longed to be able to sit comfortably, to be able to speak with Cynwrig. He needed to find out every bit of information, in order to plan ahead . . .

He was glad when Cynwrig ordered the servants to carry him to the main sleeping chamber at the far end of the hall. There he was placed on a bed of hay, covered with woollen blankets, and another folded blanket served as a pillow. Cynwrig ushered the servants away, and a curtain was drawn across the chamber's door.

'Don't! Don't draw the covering shut!'

'It will be quieter for you, my lord, shutting out the noise of the hall; the stillness will be better for you.'

'I don't want to be left; I've endured years of being alone! Oh, how I longed for company – the company of my own people; good Welshmen like you. Come and sit with me, Cynwrig. Please talk with me for a while, I have so many questions . . .' The cough engulfed his body again.

Cynwrig waited, then – 'There are others who wish to speak with you.'

'And I wish to speak . . .' more coughing, '. . . with you.'

Cynwrig smiled, then added, 'There is someone waiting to meet you, my lord.'

'Let him wait a little longer – he didn't risk his life in

Chester like you.' He spoke with a little more authority in his voice. 'Come, sit at the end of the bed here.'

The man sat. Gruffudd watched him for a while, suddenly feeling awkward. Conveying his feelings was difficult. He looked out towards the opening and beyond into the hall, where there was a little light. A servant was lighting the torches along the walls. His eyesight was better in the greyness, without the bright torches burning – but he couldn't expect the others to eat their meal in darkness. He moved his gaze again to the face in front of him. He noticed the forehead, the beard, the broad shoulders that had carried him in the sack . . .

'Don't expect me to thank you, Cynwrig Hir.'

'I expect nothing, my lord.'

'I was never any good at expressing my gratitude; I don't want to be in debt to another. Do you understand?'

'I think I understand, sir.'

Gruffudd smiled. 'I'm glad. I have so many questions.' He coughed hard again, 'You were in Rhug . . .' he paused, waiting, but Cynwrig remained silent. Gruffudd went on, 'My men? They were wounded – their thumbs were cut?'

'Yes.' The man was uneasy.

'Do you know what became of them?'

'Afterwards?'

'Yes.'

'They were free; they went back to Ireland.' Then he added quietly, 'A few refused to be defiled . . . there were skirmishes . . .'

'They were slaughtered?' Gruffudd's voice flat.

'Yes – less than twenty of them.'

'What of the others?' His voice unsteady.

During the last hours, as the miracle of being free had suddenly formed into reality, he had dared to hope for another miracle. No one had said for certain that Collwyn was dead.

'Who do you mean, my lord?'

'My officers . . . they were struck when I was there, on the meadow in Rhug . . .' He couldn't bring himself to ask directly, as if he could not bear to take the blow. 'What became of Sitriuc? Do you recall him? A giant of a man!'

'Yes I remember him, and his brother. He fell, and so did his brother. Both died before the Normans began defiling the others.'

'Both of them.' Gruffudd's voice, flat again. 'They were great men! Cormac? Do you remember Cormac?'

'He died where he fell.'

'He was cunning, always shrewd – he would have been a great advantage to us, even without the use of his bow.'

Another pause, but he had to know – 'And my great friend Collwyn?'

'Yes, your companion, I know. He was badly wounded, the Normans did their usual deed, but he was allowed to return to Anglesey with what was left of your army.'

Gruffudd sat up. 'Then he lived?'

Cynwrig paused again, choosing his words. 'He died of his wounds in Anglesey . . . before sailing for Ireland.'

Gruffudd suddenly felt cold, his body heavy and empty. He was on his back again, as if he had suffered a physical blow. Cynwrig got to his feet.

'My lord, I fear that I'm making you weak . . . and someone else is here . . .'

'Oh?' He had little interest. Glimpsing in the direction of the hall, he saw a woman standing in the opening. He realised that he had yet to meet Cynwrig's wife: of course, the man wanted him to meet her. He swung his legs to the edge of the bed, and managed with an effort to get to his feet. 'Come in!' he called.

She entered. Gruffudd noted that she was tall, her hair over her shoulders; she was beautiful.

'My lord.' The woman whispered.

A tremor went through him. 'I'm afraid . . .' he said slowly, '. . . that I'm a great burden.'

'Yes, and have been so for six years, my lord.'

'What?'

'And six years before them.'

'Who are you?' Then he turned to Cynwrig, who was leaving. 'Who is she?'

He waited, silently. The woman came to the end of the bed. 'Have I changed so?'

Immediately he knew. Elation rushed through him, suddenly changing to fear, fear turning quickly to a fierce hatred. He looked at Cynwrig, trying to control the fury in his voice. 'Take the wife of Rhuddlan's baron out of here.'

'But sir!' Cynwrig began.

'Take her away . . .' He felt his composure slipping, the cough back. 'I see nothing but treachery . . .'

Cynwrig stepped forward again. 'My lord, you must understand, it was Angharad, more than any other, who did most to save you . . .'

'No! How could you be such a fool? It will be just as it was in Rhug. She will inform the devil in Rhuddlan . . .'

'Robert is away on a mission in England,' said Angharad.

'It was Angharad who planned your escape . . .' Cynwrig went on. 'She realised what could be done, while the barons were away. She got word that you were taken out into the town, and she chose me to get you out . . .'

Gruffudd felt a strange force in him that wanted to hurt her, and Cynwrig, further.

'How could you . . . How was it that you gave this woman your trust, a woman who could abandon her lord, just because he was out of sight . . .'

'But sir, I know Angharad, I trust her . . .'

'Listen to me!' He tried to shout, but the cough made his voice small. 'You are weak! You are far too trusting of traitors – this one's husband and her cousin Meirion Goch. I'm afraid that I'll pay once more for your stupidity!' His last words drowned, Gruffudd had to lean on the wall, his whole body taken over by another bout of coughing. Cynwrig left in search of some water, his feet heavy.

They remained there, motionless. Then her voice, low but with a hint of anger – 'There. We have heard again the voice of the pirate, whose cruelty knows no bounds.' He raised his head. She went on. 'That man, he was prepared to die for you,' she sighed. 'Of course, we did not expect gratitude – we know you well enough – but we didn't expect punishment.'

He couldn't make out her face. 'What did you expect?'

She didn't answer him.

'Is this just your way of getting back at your husband for

some wrong? Or is my fate a bit of amusement for the Lady of Rhuddlan – a little excitement that you talk about with your ladies when you embroider?'

Coughing again, he leaned on the wall. Then she was by his side. 'Did you ever think that others have also suffered during those six years?'

'But you agreed to marry him?'

'Yes.'

He expected her to say that that was the price for letting him live. Was that not the truth, as Philip had said many times? She said nothing. She didn't want to take away from him his victory over them. Suddenly his rage ebbed and instead he felt a surge of tenderness towards her. She understood. 'Hold me, Gruffudd.'

He hesitated, the familiar stubbornness stopping him.

'Just once, Gruffudd.'

Slowly, he took her in his arms and held her, then he drew her towards him, pressing his face into her hair, smelling the strange perfume on her skin. Another Norman habit. The scent made him angry again.

'Even the scent of your skin reminds me of him.'

'I can wash my skin.'

'But you can't wash six years away.'

'We have years and years together . . .'

'Together – how?' He leaned back so as to have better view of her face. She raised her face to look at him.

'I can never go back to Rhuddlan.'

'You cannot come with me.' His voice certain. She took a step away from him.

'So, where shall I go Gruffudd . . . seeing as I'm of no more use to you?' It was her turn.

Gruffudd flinched, looking past her towards the hall. Servants were pushing the trestle tables into the centre of the room.

'Angharad.' For the first time he had said her name. 'Do you expect me to scamper off to Ireland, and live at the mercy of my mother's people, and take you with me? Is that what you expect me to do?'

'No.'

'What, then? That I stay in Gwynedd? A mere lord on a parcel of land in Eryri perhaps – with Robert's blessing of course, having taken his wife from him?'

She ignored the sarcasm in his words.

'You will have to find your place.' She held onto his arm. 'What if you went . . .' Then she changed her tone. 'Wherever you go, you must take me with you this time.'

Gruffudd saw the reflection of the light from the hall in her eyes.

'No – I don't need anyone but my men . . . loyal, brave men. Soldiers who will fight at my side day after day against the Normans, summer and winter, year after year, until Gwynedd is free of their clutches. Next time I will not submit – it will be death or . . .' He stopped again to take a deep breath. 'This is my kingdom – Gwynedd belongs to me and my people.'

'Yes Gruffudd,' her voice tender. 'Would I be a hindrance?'

'You know that.'

'Yes.' Gruffudd stroked her hair, gently. 'Then where should I go?'

The servants were preparing for the feast, placing dishes on the tables. Gruffudd could hear the wooden plates on the rough boards, one of the servants whistling, firewood crackling. He could not see the fire, but on the opposite wall he could see the reflection of the flames rising. He recalled a fire somewhere else . . . at the great hall in Rhuddlan.

'Stay here. Cynwrig will accompany me. Will you remain with his wife and keep her company?'

'And then?'

'Then? Well, you won't have to choose – there will only be one of us living in Gwynedd – me or Robert.'

'What?' she looked at him again, her face dark, troubled, as if she had not contemplated precisely what his freedom could mean. In that instant she seemed so young and innocent.

He was tired. 'Pray for the right one, won't you!' he said lightly, seeing the tears in her eyes.

'I don't find it amusing, I cannot jest . . .'

'And I cannot cry . . .'

They both stayed there, still, silent.

'And what will become of me?

'If I'm the one who is left standing?'

'Yes.'

'And not a Norman left in Gwynedd?'

'Yes.'

Gruffudd became aware of the smell of meat roasting, the sound of merriment, a dog hurtled past the opening . . . He smiled. 'What will become of you? Ah, well, the King of Gwynedd will be joining you at the altar in the great Church of St. Deiniol in Bangor.'

She moved towards him, grasping his hands. He took her in his arms, kissing her lightly. They remained in each other's arms for a while. Then Gruffudd realised that Cynwrig was standing in the hall, just outside the opening. He whispered, 'Being able to hold you like this is like holding on to life. I'm getting stronger, but not strong enough yet to stay on my feet – even to hold on to the finest treasure. Let me sit down!'

She jumped back. 'I'm sorry, I didn't think . . .'

He sat back down on the bed. 'Cynwrig has brought me a drink . . .'

'I'll stay at your side; I don't want to feast . . .'

'No, you must accompany the lady of the house. I need to talk to Cynwrig, to arrange for you to stay. I need to know what the situation is in Gwynedd . . . I need to plan ahead.'

'Tonight?'

'I need to take leadership . . .'

'Very well.' Trying to hide her disappointment, she took hold of his hand once more. 'Your hand,' she said, 'what is it?'

'A little blood.' He smiled. 'When you grasped my hand – the wound made by the shackles – it reopens. I have an order,' he said. 'An important one. You must . . .'

Angharad looked at him, her eyes solemn. 'What is it?'

'You must care for me each day for a month – or until I'm strong again.' She smiled and bowed to kiss his face.

'No one else will be allowed near you!'

Then she turned to leave as Cynwrig entered carrying another basin.

'Here, some milk,' he said, passing Gruffudd the bowl. 'They've mixed in some eggs for extra nourishment.'

Gruffudd took the offered vessel, and drank. 'When can I take some meat?'

'In three days, my lord. Is the smell of the beef too tempting?'

'Yes!' he laughed.

A few men passed by the opening and sat at the tables. Cynwrig watched as Gruffudd drank.

'My lord, are you willing to come to the feast? Just to make a short appearance at the end?'

'Yes, just for a minute or two . . . I'm very tired.'

'It's the relief that things worked out, sir; so much has happened in just one day . . .'

Gruffudd laughed again. 'I can hardly believe it! Tell me – was Gamaches slain?'

'Who?'

'The tall soldier.'

'Yes. Both were killed; a blade through the heart – there was no other way.'

'Of course.'

'The tall one – he was strong, he had weight, was he cruel?'

'No, he wasn't the worst. But he was the enemy.' Gruffudd drank again, wiping his beard with the back of his hand, then he lay back. 'Cynwrig, I would like it if Angharad could stay here until I get my kingdom together . . .'

'Of course – she can make here her home. She will be safe.'

'She can be your wife's companion? While you join me in battle – it might take some time . . .'

'My lord, it will take years.'

'Why?'

'The Normans have plundered Gwynedd, my lord, leaving

no stone unturned, or any village untouched by hunger and grief, leaving nothing but desolation.' He sighed, and chose his next words carefully. 'Your kingdom is withering away under Robert's steely grip. He was given the right, they say, by the old king to call himself Prince of Gwynedd.'

'A Norman baron – King of Gwynedd?!' Gruffudd sat up once more. 'Given the right by who? Not by me!'

'My lord, he's building his castles – a large building has just gone up in Deganwy.'

'Deganwy?' This time Gruffudd got to his feet. 'We'll attack that first!' But the cough returned, forcing him to take to his bed.

Cynwrig came to his side. 'My lord, I should not be telling you this: you should rest; it would be best if you don't appear . . .'

'Where are they least powerful?'

'Llŷn and Anglesey.'

'Who have we left in Anglesey?'

Cynwrig hesitated. 'There is one, I hear, who troubles them, and has done so for several years – Gwyncu ap . . . ap . . .'

'Gwyncu! He's alive! I will go to him, I can recuperate there. I must get a ship! The island – a safe place to hide . . .' his words becoming almost incomprehensible, '. . . the sea, the sea, I'll be safe, I can gather men, the sea will be my protector. You will come with me . . .'

'Forgive me, sir – we would go there and leave the women behind?'

Gruffudd stared at him – 'No! They will be safer on Anglesey. We'll take them with us!' Then a horn sounded.

'You must go!' said Gruffudd. 'You and the others deserve a feast!'

'Thank you, my lord. Try and sleep for a while; I'll be back later.'

Gruffudd watched as Cynwrig returned to the hall. A row of men sat with their backs to the chamber. Gruffudd could see nothing past them, but he could hear the sound of women's voices, sometimes the sound of children at play. Another blast of the horn, the dog hurtling past again, laughter and merriment.

Pain stabbed the bottom of his spine, the cough making his head ache. He lay on his bed looking at the ceiling. He was tired, almost blind, his breath shallow and quick, he walked like a frail old man, the shackles yet to be removed gnawing at his skin . . . These were serious failings in one who dreamed of capturing a kingdom – one with only a handful of loyal men. But he had Gwyncu, and he knew that Gwynedd was rightly his . . .

He got up slowly, dragging himself along the walls, until he reached the opening. Heat from the fire warmed his face, the smell of meat, sweat and smoke. The torches and flames made his eyes hurt. All around him were hazy greyish-yellow shapes. Voices shouting, he stood unnoticed . . .

Suddenly the hall was silent, as if an order had been given. Then the forms in front of him got to their feet; the sound of feet moving, trestles being pushed aside. A voice sounded out, 'Welcome back, King!' The hall erupted in shouts and cheers – a horn sounding, and another – then words stringed together – a chant – 'Gruffudd ap Cynan, King of Gwynedd!

Gruffudd ap Cynan, King of Gwynedd, King of Gwynedd, King of Gwynedd!'

The hall swayed around him; his head reeled. He raised his hand and they became silent. His legs shook, and his head drooped. He forced his head up and shouted, 'Very soon, my people, I will be able to see you all, to face the sun once more, to climb with you my friends . . .'

His head dropped again, and a tall form rushed forward. He was aware that Angharad was also by his side. Someone held him, 'I'm afraid that you might fall . . .' Cynwrig's voice.

Then Angharad – 'Come, you must rest.'

'But I haven't reassured them . . .'

'There is plenty of time.'

'But not another day such as this.' Gruffudd raised his head again, arms holding him up. 'Give me a moment.' Then his voice gained strength – 'Who will join me? We'll demolish the castle . . .' another fit of coughing, 'Deganwy Castle in the new year, and then . . . Rhuddlan . . . and then Chester!'

He was carried back into his room, the shouts of the men ringing in his ears.

When the cough had eased, he lay on his bed. Sleep would not come; his mind was too full of plans. His eyes shut; he became aware of the sounds of the feasting. He was glad he had appeared in the hall, just to feel the support – he had needed to hear them shout out his name . . . now he could begin to make his plans.

He would need Cynwrig Hir; he was loyal and wise. He had depended heavily on Collwyn; no-one could take his place, but he needed a comrade, someone whom he could rely on –

a brother, friend and servant. He needed Cynwrig by his side.

He became aware that Angharad had moved from the foot of the bed. Her voice very near, her hair on his face, he could feel the warmth of her body. He didn't move his arms to hold her, his tiredness taking over. He dreamt of being on a ship sailing down Afon Menai, Cynwrig Hir by his side. They were heading for Deganwy . . .

'Can you still smell the scent?'

'No.'

She whispered, 'I washed it off . . .'

'Good!' He took a deep breath. 'I smell the sea breeze on your skin; it reminds me of the time you came to Aberffraw.'

He became conscious of her moving away from him.

'That's all I needed to hear . . . I'll let you sleep.'

He heard the curtain being drawn across the opening.

He said nothing, then she was gone. His mind slipped back to the ship. On it were the best men from Anglesey and Llŷn – Gwyncu was there of course, as was Cynwrig Hir . . . a few Irishmen, their axes ready . . . But sleep overcame him before he reached Deganwy.

List of Place Names

Môn – Anglesey
Gwynedd
Eryri
Llŷn
Eifionydd
Arfon
Rhufoniog
Edeyrnion
Tegeingl
Perfeddwlad
Maelor
Mercia

Powys

Aberffraw
Rhosyr
Afon Menai
Bangor

Rhuddlan
Deganwy
Rhug
Malpas
Northop

Chester
Shrewsbury
Montgomery
Severn Valley

Dublin
Sord-Cholum-Cille (near Dublin)
Port Láirge – Waterford
Leinster
Saltee Islands

Gwaed Erw
Bron yr Erw (Battles)
Mynydd Carn

Normandy
Rouen

Gruffudd ap Cynan (1055-1137)

A short history

Imagine the scene: on a headland not far from Dublin, a mother and her young son look out to sea. On the horizon, they can make out a range of mountains.

'Gwynedd,' she tells her son. 'There is your father's kingdom – *teyrnas* Cynan. He had to flee, leaving his kingdom – but one day you will return. You will become King of Gwynedd!'

Gruffudd ap Cynan's father had died as an exile in Dublin – a city occupied by the Danes – and Rhagnell, his mother, was a Dane. Wales was under threat from another force. In 1066 the Normans had landed in Hastings, conquering the Anglo-Saxons in an afternoon. It took another two hundred years for them to lay their claim on Wales. However, they gradually ventured from their English castles, edging their way further into Welsh lands, establishing forts along the border. The castle at Chester to the North became a Norman stronghold, threatening the kingdom of Gwynedd.

With the support of the Irish and Danes of Dublin, Gruffudd secured men and ships to help him establish himself in Gwynedd. It was a turbulent age, marked by vicious battles, rivalry among the Welsh kings and the deception and cruelty of the Normans. For over a quarter of a century, Gruffudd ap Cynan landed and retreated, regaining land and support in Wales, before vanishing again to the safety of Ireland. But he did not give up.

He secured a faithful following, as the novel shows. The Normans tricked him into attending a meeting in Rhug: a meeting supposedly to discuss peace, only for him to be captured in a terrible ruse and held prisoner at Chester for twelve years. He kept his dream alive, and when he was at last able to escape his tormentors, he showed great tenacity and resolve to carry on in spite of many setbacks. He showed great wisdom, courage and a drive to fight on. He eventually became one of the most successful Welsh kings of all time, driving the Normans from Gwynedd, demolishing their castles. Apart from one year, 1098-99, he ruled Gwynedd for 40 years, establishing a strong kingdom. Among his descendants were many great leaders, namely Owain Gwynedd, Llywelyn the Great, Llywelyn ab Iorwerth and Owain Glyndŵr. There is no doubt that Gwynedd, Gruffudd's kingdom, led the Welsh people in their quest to maintain their independence in the face of Norman attack.

During this eventful period, as he fought to re-establish himself in his father's kingdom, Gruffudd married Angharad, a noblewoman from north-west Wales. Gruffudd ap Cynan is the only Welsh king or prince who has his life recorded in a memoir dating from the Middle Ages. In it, Angharad is praised for her wisdom, eloquence, generosity and beauty. She stood by her husband through challenging times, and they had three sons and five daughters.

One daughter was Gwenllian, who married Gruffudd ap Rhys, the leader of the Welsh in Deheubarth (south-west Wales). In 1136, while her husband's army was away, she led a legion of farmers and tenants from Deheubarth against a

Norman army near the castle of Cydweli. The Welsh lost the battle. One of her sons was killed in battle and Gwenllian and another son were both executed on the battlefield, after the fighting had ceased. The news of Gwenllian and her son's treatment further enraged the Welsh, resulting in Gruffudd ap Cynan, his sons and the men of Gwynedd rallying to the aid of Deheubarth.

The Normans were defeated in the battle of Crug Mawr, near Aberteifi (Cardigan), and within twelve months, not one Norman or Norman castle stood to the west of the Nedd river. Gruffudd ap Cynan travelled from Gwynedd to the Tywi valley to celebrate the victory with members of his family.

Following his death in 1137, he was buried in Bangor Cathedral in a remarkable ceremony, where he was lauded as the leader who had defended and brought peace to Wales. Despite all the problems and conflicts he endured, his journey from a boy in Dublin to his position as King of Gwynedd was an astounding accomplishment. Furthermore, he succeeded in developing agriculture, and among the arts he gave poetry a prominent place. He demonstrated that the Welsh should not fear the Normans – that standing with courage and solidarity is the way to prevail and conquer.

Thanks from Anne & Owen Wyn Roberts:-

Myrddin ap Dafydd for his advice, guidance, and assistance;
Gwasg Carreg Gwalch for publication;
Haf Llewelyn for her wonderful translation skills;
Brian Dutton for his untiring assistance and advice;
Awen Hamilton Llanystumdwy for advice and assistance.

Novels steeped in history

Exciting and subtle stories based on key historical events

Winner of the 2014 Tir na-nOg award in the original Welsh

THE DARKEST OF DAYS
Gareth F. Williams

A novel based on the Senghennydd disaster 1913

£5.99

Shortly before 8.30 on the morning of 14 October 1913, 439 men and boys perished in a horrific explosion at Senghennydd coal mine.

John Williams was only eight years old when he and his family came from one of the slate mining villages of the north to live in Senghennydd, in the South Wales valleys. He looked forward to his thirteenth birthday, when he too would commence work in the coal mine. But he was unaware of the black cloud that was heading towards Senghennydd ...

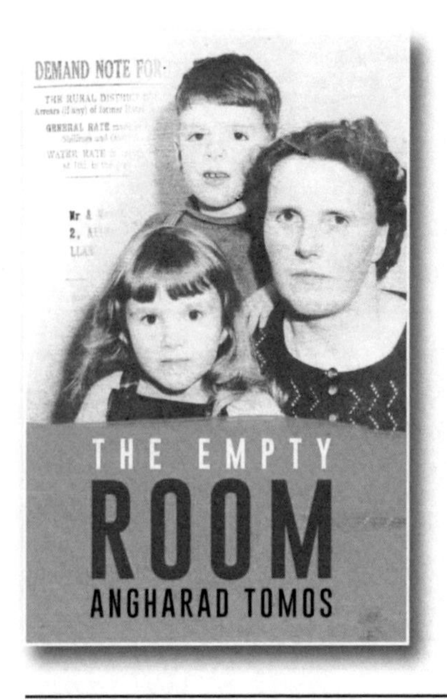

THE EMPTY ROOM
Angharad Tomos

A Welsh family's fight for a basic human right 1952-1960

£5.99

Shortlisted
for the 2015
Tir na-nOg award
in the original
Welsh

THE IRON DAM
Myrddin ap Dafydd

A novel full of excitement and bravery about ordinary people battling for their area's future.

£5.99

Shortlisted
for the 2017
Tir na-nOg award
in the original
Welsh

THE MOON IS RED
Myrddin ap Dafydd

Fire at a Bombing School in Llŷn in 1936 and bombs raining down on the city of Gernika in the Basque Country during the Spanish Civil War – and one family's story woven through all of this.

£6.99

Winner of the 2018 Tir na-nOg award in the original Welsh

UNDER THE WELSH NOT
Myrddin ap Dafydd

"you'll get a beating for speaking Welsh ..."

Bob starts at Ysgol y Llan at the end of the summer, but he's worried. He doesn't have a word of English. The 'Welsh Not' stigma for speaking Welsh is still used at that school.

£7.50

THE CROWN IN THE QUARRY
Myrddin ap Dafydd

The world's largest diamond ... in Blaenau Ffestiniog

The story of evacuees and moving London's treasures to the safety of the quarries during the Second World War.

£7

THE BLACK PIT OF TONYPANDY
Myrddin ap Dafydd

It is 1910, a turbulent time of disputes, strikes and riots in Cwm Rhondda, when the miners are fighting for fair wages and better working conditions.

People from different backgrounds are thrown together, resulting in friendships and conflict ...

£7.99